The Boss of Taroomba by E. W. Hornung

Ernest William Hornung was born in Middlesbrough, England on 7th June 1866, the third son and youngest of eight children.

Although spending most of his life in England and France he spent two years in Australia from 1884 and that experience was to colour and influence much of his written works.

His most famous character A. J. Raffles, 'the gentleman thief', was published first in Cassell's Magazine during 1898 and was to make him famous across the world as the new century dawned.

Hornung also wrote several stage plays and was a gifted poet.

Spending time with the troops in WWI he published Notes of a Camp-Follower on the Western Front during 1919, a detailed account of his time there. This was especially close to his heart as his son, and only child, was killed at the Second Battle of Ypres on 6th July 1915.

Ernest William Hornung died in Saint-Jean-de-Luz, in the south of France on 22nd March 1921.

Index of Contents

I0553641

CHAPTER I

THE LITTLE MUSICIAN

They were terribly sentimental words, but the fellow sang them as though he meant every syllable. Altogether, the song was not the kind of thing to go down with a back-block audience, any more than the singer was the class of man.

He was a little bit of a fellow, with long dark hair and dark glowing eyes, and he swayed on the music-stool, as he played and sang, in a manner most new to the young men of Taroomba. He had not much voice, but the sensitive lips took such pains with each word, and the long, nervous fingers fell so lightly upon the old piano, that every one of the egregious lines travelled whole and unmistakable to the farthest corner of the room. And that was an additional pity, because the piano was so placed that the performer was forced to turn his back upon his audience; and behind it the young men of Taroomba were making great game of him all the time.

In the moderate light of two kerosene lamps, the room seemed full of cord breeches and leather belts and flannel collars and sunburnt throats. It was not a large room, however, and there were only four men present, not counting the singer. They were young fellows, in the main, though the one leaning his elbow on the piano had a bushy red beard, and his yellow hair was beginning to thin. Another was reading The Australasian on the sofa; and a sort of twist to his mustache, a certain rigor about his unshaven chin, if they betrayed no sympathy with the singer, suggested a measure of contempt for the dumb clownery going on behind the singer's back. Over his very head, indeed, the red-bearded man was signalling maliciously to a youth who with coarse fat face and hands was mimicking the performer in the middle of the room; while the youngest man of the lot, who wore spectacles and a Home-bred look, giggled in a half-ashamed, half-anxious way, as though not a little concerned lest they should all be caught. And when the song ended, and the singer spun round on the stool, they had certainly a narrow escape.

"Great song!" cried the mimic, pulling himself together in an instant, and clapping out a brutal burlesque of applause.

"Shut up, Sandy," said the man with the beard, dropping a yellow-fringed eyelid over a very blue eye. "Don't you mind Mr. Sanderson, sir," he added to the musician; "he's not a bad chap, only he thinks he's funny. We'll show him what funniment really is in a minute or two. I've just found the very song! But what's the price of the last pretty thing?"

"Of 'Love Flees before the Dawn?'" said the musician, simply.

"Yes."

"It's the same as all the rest; you see—"

Here the mimic broke in with a bright, congenial joke.

"Love how much?" cried he, winking with his whole heavy face. "I don't, chaps, do you?"

The sally was greeted with a roar, in which the musician joined timidly, while the man on the sofa smiled faintly without looking up from his paper.

"Never mind him," said the red-bearded man, who was for keeping up the fun as long as possible; "he's too witty to live. What did you say the price was?"

"Most of the songs are half a crown."

"Come, I say, that's a stiffish price, isn't it?"

"Plucky stiff for fleas!" exclaimed the wit.

The musician flushed, but tossed back his head of hair, and held out his hand for the song.

"I can't help it, gentlemen. I can't afford to charge less. Every one of these songs has been sent out from Home, and I get them from a man in Melbourne, who makes me pay for them. You're five hundred miles up country, where you can't expect town prices."

"Keep your hair on, old man!" said the wit, soothingly.

"My what? My hair is my own business!"

The little musician had turned upon his tormentor like a knife. His dark eyes were glaring indignantly, and his nervous fingers had twitched themselves into a pair of absurdly unserviceable white fists. But now a freckled hand was laid upon his shoulder, and the man with the beard was saying, "Come, come, my good fellow, you've made a mistake; my friend Sanderson meant nothing personal. It's our way up here, you know, to chi-ak each other and our visitors too."

"Then I don't like your way," said the little man, stoutly.

"Well, Sandy meant no offence, I'll swear to that."

"Of course I didn't," said Sanderson.

The musician looked from one to the other, and the anger went out of him, making way for shame.

"Then the offence is on my side," said he, awkwardly, "and I beg your pardon."

He took a pile of new music from the piano, and was about to go.

"No, no, we're not going to let you off so easily," said the bearded man, laughing.

"You'll have to sing us one more song to show there's no ill feeling," put in Sanderson.

"And here's the song," added the other. "The very thing. I found it just now. There you are—'The World's Creation!'"

"Not that thing!" said the musician.

"Why not?"

"It's a comic song."

"The very thing we want."

"We'll buy up your whole stock of comic songs," said Sanderson.

"Hear, hear," cried the silent youth who wore spectacles.

"I wish you would," the musician said, smiling.

"But we must hear them first."

"I hate singing them."

"Well, give us this one as a favor! Only this one. Do."

The musician wavered. He was a very sensitive young man, with a constitutional desire to please, and an acute horror of making a fool of himself. Now the whole soul of him was aching with the conviction that he had done this already, in showing his teeth at what had evidently been meant as harmless and inoffensive badinage. And it was this feeling that engendered the desperate desire at once to expiate his late display of temper, and to win the good opinion of these men by fairly amusing them after all. Certainly the song in demand did not amuse himself, but then it was equally certain that his taste in humor differed from theirs. He could not decide in his mind. He longed to make these men laugh. To get on with older and rougher men was his great difficulty, and one of his ambitions.

"We must have this," said the man with the beard, who had been looking over the song. "The words are first chop!"

"I can't stand them," the musician confessed.

"Why, are they too profane?"

"They are too silly."

"Well, they ain't for us. Climb down to our level, and fire away."

With a sigh and a smile, and a full complement of those misgivings which were a part of his temperament, the little visitor sat down and played with much vivacity a banjo accompaniment which sounded far better than anything else had done on the antiquated, weather-beaten bush piano. The jingle struck fire with the audience, and the performer knew it, as he went on to describe himself as "straight from Old Virginia," with his head "stuffed full of knowledge," in spite of the fact that he had "never been to 'Frisco or any other college;" the entertaining information that "this world it was created in the twinkling of two cracks" bringing the first verse to a conclusion. Then came the chorus—of which there can scarcely be two opinions. The young men caught it up with a howl, with the exception of the reader on the sofa, who put his fingers in his ears. This is how it went:

Oh, walk up, Mr. Pompey, oh, walk up while I say,
Will you walk into the banjo and hear the parlor play?
Will you walk into the parlor and hear the banjo ring?
Oh, listen to de darkies how merrily dey sing!

The chorus ended with a whoop which assured the soloist that he was amusing his men; and having himself one of those susceptible, excitable natures which can enter into almost anything, given the fair wind of appreciation to fill their sails, the little musician began actually to enjoy the nonsense himself. His long fingers rang out the tinkling accompaniment with a crisp, confident touch. He sang the second verse, which built up the universe in numbers calculated to shock a religious or even a reasonably cultivated order of mind, as though he were by no means ashamed of it. And so far as culture and religion were concerned he was tolerably safe—each fresh peal of laughter reassured him of this. That the laugh was with him he never doubted until the end of the third verse. Then it was that the roars of merriment rose louder than ever, and that their note suddenly struck the musician's trained ear as false. He sang through the next verse with an overwhelming sense of its inanity, and with the life gone out of his voice and fingers alike. Still they roared with laughter, but he who made them knew now that the laugh was at his expense. He turned hot all over, then cold, then hotter than ever. A shadow was dancing on the music in front of him; he could hear a suppressed titter at the back of the boisterous laughter; something brushed against his hair, and he could bear it all no longer. Snatching his fingers from the keys, he wheeled round on the music-stool in time to catch the heavy youth Sanderson in the mimic act of braining him with a chair; his tongue was out like a brat's, his eyes shone with a baleful mirth, while the red-bearded man was rolling about the room in an ecstasy of malicious merriment.

The singer sprang to his feet in a palsy of indignation. His dark eyes glared with the dumb rage of a wounded animal; then they ranged round the room for something with which to strike, and before Sanderson had time to drop the chair he had been brandishing over the other's head, the musician had snatched up the kerosene lamp from the top of the piano, and was poising it in the air with murderous intent. Yet his anger had not blinded him utterly. His flashing eyes were fixed upon the fat mocking face which he longed to mark for life, but he could also see beyond it, and what he saw made him put down the lamp without a word.

At the other side of the room was a door leading out upon the veranda; it had been open all the evening, and now it was the frame of an unlooked-for picture, for a tall, strong girl was standing upon the threshold.

"Well, I never!" said she, calmly, as she came into their midst with a slow, commanding stride. "So this is the way you play when I'm away, is it? What poor little mice they are, to be sure!"

Sanderson had put down the chair, and was looking indescribably foolish. The boy in the spectacles, though he had been a merely passive party to the late proceedings, seemed only a little less uncomfortable. The man on the sofa and the little trembling musician were devouring the girl with their eyes. It was the personage with the beard who swaggered forward into the breach.

"Good-evening, Naomi," said he, holding out a hand which she refused to see. "This is Mr. Engelhardt, who has come to tune your piano for you. Mr. Engelhardt—Miss Pryse."

The hand which had been refused to the man who was in a position to address Miss Pryse as Naomi, was held out frankly to the stranger. It was a firm, cool hand, which left him a stronger and a saner man for its touch.

"I am delighted to see you, Mr. Engelhardt. I congratulate you on your songs, and on your spirit, too. It was about time that Mr. Sanderson met somebody who objected to his peculiar form of fun. He has been spoiling for this ever since I have known him!"

"Come, I say, Naomi," said the man who was on familiar terms with her, "it was all meant in good part, you know. You're rather rough upon poor Sandy."

"Not so rough as both you and he have been upon a visitor. I am ashamed of you all!"

Her scornful eyes looked black in the lamplight; her eyebrows were black. This with her splendid coloring was all the musician could be sure of; though his gaze never shifted from her face. Now she turned to him and said, kindly:

"I have been enjoying your songs immensely—especially the comic one. I came in some time ago, and have been listening to everything. You sing splendidly."

"These gentlemen will hardly agree with you."

"These gentlemen," said Miss Pryse, laying an unpleasant stress on the word, "disagree with me horribly at times. They make me ill. What a lot of songs you have brought!"

"I brought them to sell," said the young fellow, blushing. "I have just started business—set up shop at Deniliquin—a music-shop, you know. I am making a round to tune the pianos at the stations."

"What a capital idea! You will find ours in a terrible state, I'm afraid."

"Yes, it is rather bad; I was talking about it to the boss before I started to make a fool of myself."

"To the boss, do you say?"

"Yes."

"And pray which is he?"

The piano-tuner pointed to the bushy red beard.

"Why, bless your life," cried Naomi Pryse, as the red beard split across and showed its teeth, "he's not the boss! Don't you believe it. If you've anything to say to the boss, you'd better come outside and say it."

"But which is he, Miss Pryse?"

"He's a she, and you're talking to her now, Mr. Engelhardt!"

CHAPTER II

A FRIEND INDEED

"Do you mean to say that you have never heard of the female boss of Taroomba?" said Naomi Pryse, as she led the piano-tuner across the veranda and out into the station-yard. The moon was gleaming upon the galvanized-iron roofs of the various buildings, and it picked out the girl's smile as she turned to question her companion.

"No, I never heard of you before," replied the piano-tuner, stolidly. For the moment the girl and the moonlight stupefied him. The scene in the room was still before his eyes and in his ears.

"Well, that's one for me! What station have you come from to-day?"

"Kerulijah."

"And you never heard of me there! Ah, well, I'm very seldom up here. I've only come for the shearing. Still, the whole place is mine, and I'm not exactly a cipher in the business either; I rather thought I was the talk of the back-blocks. At one time I know I was. I'm very vain, you see."

"You have something to be vain about," said the piano-tuner, looking at her frankly.

She made him a courtesy in the moonlit yard.

"Thank you kindly. But I'm not satisfied yet; I understand that you arrived in time for supper; didn't you hear of me at table?"

"I just heard your name."

"Who mentioned it?"

"The fellow with the beard."

"Prettily?"

"I think so. He was wondering where you were. He seems to know you very well?"

"He has known me all my life. He is a sort of connection. He was overseer here when my father died a year or two ago. He is the manager now."

"But you are the boss?"

"I am so! His name, by the way, is Gilroy—my mother was a Gilroy, too. See? That's why he calls me Naomi; I call him Monty when I am not wroth with him. I am disgusted with them all to-night! But you mustn't mind them; it's only their way. Did you speak to the overseer, Tom Chester?"

"Which was he?"

"The one on the sofa."

"No, he hardly spoke to me."

"Well, he's a very good sort; you would like him if you got to know him. The new chum with the eye-glasses is all right, too. I don't believe those two were to blame. As for Mr. Sanderson, I wouldn't think any more about him if I were you; he really isn't worth it."

"I forgive him," said the musician, simply; "but I shall never forgive myself for playing the fool and losing my temper!"

"Nonsense! It did them good, and they'll think all the more of you. Still, I must say I'm glad you didn't dash the kerosene lamp in Mr. Sanderson's face!"

"The what?" cried Engelhardt, in horror.

"The lamp; you were brandishing it over your head when I came in."

"The lamp! To think that I caught up the lamp! I can't have known what I was doing!"

He stood still and aghast in the sandy yard; they had wandered to the far side of it, where the kitchen and the laundry stood cheek-by-jowl with the wood-heap between them, and their back-walls to the six-wire fence dividing the yard from the plantation of young pines which bordered it upon three sides.

"You were in a passion," said Miss Pryse, smiling gravely. "There's nothing in this world that I admire more than a passion—it's so uncommon. So are you! There, I owed you a pretty speech, you know! Do you mind giving me your arm, Mr. Engelhardt?"

But Engelhardt was gazing absently at the girl, and the road between ear and mind was choked with a multitude of new sensations. Her sudden request made no impression upon him, until he saw her stamping her foot in the sand. Then, and awkwardly enough, he held out his arm to her, and her firm hand caught in it impatiently.

"How slow you are to assist a lady! Yet I feel sure that you come from the old country?"

"I do; but I have never had much to do with ladies."

The piano-tuner sighed.

"Well, it's all right; only I wanted you to take my arm for Monty Gilroy's benefit. He's just come out on to the veranda. Don't look round. This will rile him more than anything."

"But why?"

"Why? Oh, because he showed you the hoof; and when a person does that, he never likes to see another person being civil to the same person. See? Then if you don't, you'd better stand here and work it out while I run into the kitchen to speak to Mrs. Potter about your room."

"But I'm not going to stay!" the piano-tuner cried, excitedly.

"Now what are you giving us, Mr. Engelhardt? Of course you are going to stay. You're going to stay and tune my poor old piano. Why, your horse was run out hours ago!"

"But I can't face those men again—"

"What rubbish!"

"After the way I made a fool of myself this evening!"

"It was they who made fools of themselves. They'll annoy you no more, I promise you. In any case, they all go back to the shed to-morrow evening; it's seven miles away, and they only come in for Sunday. You needn't start on the piano before Monday, if you don't like."

"Oh, no, I'll do it to-morrow," Engelhardt said, moodily. He now felt bitterly certain that he should never make friends with the young men of Taroomba, and shamefully thankful to think that there would be a set occupation to keep him out of their way for the whole of the morrow.

"Very well, then; wait where you are for two twos."

Engelhardt waited. The kitchen-door had closed upon Miss Naomi Pryse; there was no sense in watching that any longer. So the piano-tuner's eyes climbed over the waterspout, scaled the steep corrugated roof, and from the wide wooden chimney leapt up to the moon. It was at the full. The white clear light hit the young man between his expressive eyes, and still he chose to face it. It gave to the delicate eager face an almost ethereal pallor; and as he gazed on without flinching, the raised head was proudly carried, and the little man looked tall. To one whom he did not hear when she lifted the kitchen-latch and opened the door, he seemed a different being; she watched him for some moments before she spoke.

"Well, Mr. Engelhardt?"

"Well," said he, coming down from the moon with an absent smile, and slowly.

"I have been watching you for quite a minute. I believe it would have been an hour if I hadn't spoken. I wish I hadn't! We're going to put you in that little building over there—we call it the 'barracks.' You'll be next door to Tom Chester, and he'll take care of you. There's no occasion to thank me; you can tell me what you've been thinking about instead."

"I wasn't thinking at all."

"Now, Mr. Engelhardt!" said Naomi, holding up her finger reprovingly. "If you weren't thinking, I should like to know what you were doing?"

"I was waiting for you."

"I know you were. It was very good of you. But you were smiling, too, and I want to know the joke."

"Was I really smiling?"

"Haven't I told you so? Have you signed the pledge against smiles? You look glum enough for anything now."

"Yes?"

"Very much yes! I wish to goodness you'd smile again."

"Oh, I'll do anything you like." He forced up the corners of his mouth, but it was not a smile; his eyes ran into hers like bayonets.

"Then give me your arm again," she said, "and let me tell you that I'm very much surprised at you for requiring to be told that twice."

"I'm not accustomed to ladies," Engelhardt explained once more.

"That's all right. I'm not one, you know. I'm going to negotiate this fence. Will you have the goodness to turn your back?"

Engelhardt did so, and saw afar off in the moonlit veranda the lowering solitary figure of the manager, Gilroy.

"Yes, he sees us all right," Miss Pryse remarked from the other side of the fence. "It'll do him good. Come you over, and we'll make his beard curl!"

The piano-tuner looked at her doubtfully, but only for one moment. The next he also was over the fence and by her side, and she was leading him into the heart of the pines, her strong kind hand within his arm.

"We'll just have a little mouch round," she said, confidentially. "You needn't be frightened."

"Frightened!" he echoed, defiantly. The hosts of darkness could not have frightened such a voice.

"You see, I'm the boss, and I'm obliged to show it sometimes."

"I see."

"And you have given me an opportunity of showing it pretty plainly."

"Oh!"

"Consequently, I'm very much obliged to you; and I do hope you don't mind helping me to shock Monty Gilroy?"

"I am proud."

But the kick had gone out of his voice, and to her hand his arm was suddenly as a log of wood. She mused a space. Then—

"It isn't everyone I would ask to help me in such—in such a delicate matter," she said, in a troubled tone. "You see I am a woman at the mercy of men. They're all very kind and loyal in their own way, but their way is their own, as you know. I thought as I had given you a hand with them—well, I thought you would be in sympathy."

"I am, I am—Heaven knows!"

The log had become exceedingly alive.

"Then let us skirt in and out, on the edge of the plantation, so that Mr. Gilroy may have the pleasure of seeing my frock from time to time."

"I'm your man."

"No, not that way—this. There, I'm sure he must have seen me then."

"He must."

"It's time we went back; but this will have done him all the good in the world," said Naomi.

"It's a pity you haven't a manager whom you can respect and like," the piano-tuner remarked.

Naomi started. She also stopped to lace up her shoe, which necessitated the withdrawal of her hand from the piano-tuner's arm; and she did not replace it.

"Oh, but I do like him, Mr. Engelhardt," she explained as she stooped. "I like Mr. Gilroy very much; I have known him all my life, you know. However, that's just where the disadvantage comes in—he's too much inclined to domineer. But don't you run away with the idea that I dislike him; that would never do at all."

The piano-tuner felt too small to apologize. He had made a deadly mistake—so bad a one that she would take his arm no more. He looked up at the moon with miserable eyes, and his brain teemed with bitter self-upbraiding thoughts. His bitterness was egregiously beyond the mark; but that was this young man's weakness. He would condemn himself to execution for the pettiest sin. So ashamed was he now that he dared not even offer her his hand when they got back to the veranda, and she consigned him to the boy in spectacles, who then showed him his room in the barracks. And his mistake kept him awake more than half that night; it was only in the gray morning he found consolation in recollecting that although she had declared so many times that she liked Monty Gilroy, she had never once said she respected him.

Had he heard a conversation which took place in the station-yard later that night, but only a little later, and while the full moon was in much the same place, the piano-tuner might have gone to sleep instead of lying awake to flagellate his own meek spirit; though it is more likely that he would have lain quietly awake for very joy. The conversation in question was between Naomi Pryse and Montague Gilroy, her manager, and it would scarcely repay a detailed report; but this is how it culminated:

"I tell you that I found you bullying him abominably, and whenever I find you bullying anybody I'll make it up to that body in my own way. And I won't have my way criticised by you."

"Very good, Naomi. Very good indeed! But if you want to guard against all chance of the same thing happening next week, I should recommend you to be in for supper next Saturday, instead of gallivanting about the run by yourself and coming in at ten o'clock at night."

"The run is mine, and I'll do what I like while I'm here."

"Well, if you won't listen to reason, you might at least remember our engagement."

"You mean your engagement? I remember the terms perfectly. I have only to write you a check for the next six months' salary any time I like, to put an end to it. And upon my word, Monty, you seem to want me to do so to-night!"

CHAPTER III

"HARD TIMES"

It was the middle of the Sunday afternoon, when the young men of Taroomba were for the most part sound asleep upon their beds. They were wise young men enough, in ways, and to punctuate the weeks of hard labor at the wool-shed with thoroughly slack Sundays at the home station was a practice of the plainest common-sense. To do otherwise would have been to fly in the face of nature. Yet just because Naomi Pryse chose to settle herself in the veranda outside the sitting-room door with a book, the young man who had worked harder than any of the others during the week must needs be the one to spend the afternoon of rest at her feet, and with nothing but a lean veranda-post to shelter his broad back from the sun.

This was Tom Chester, of whom Naomi had spoken highly to her protégé, the piano-tuner. Tom was newly and beautifully shaved, and he had further observed the Sabbath by putting on a white shirt and collar, and a suit of clothes in which a man might have walked down Collins Street; but he seemed quite content to sit in them on the dirty veranda boards, for the sake of watching Naomi as she read. She had not a great deal to say to him, but she had commanded him to light his pipe, and as often as she dropped the book into her lap to make a remark, she could reckon upon a sympathetic answer, preceded by a puff of the tobacco-smoke she loved.

"It is a dreadful noise, though, isn't it?" Naomi had observed more than once.

"It is so," Tom Chester would answer, with a smile and another puff.

"He made such a point of setting to work this morning, you know, and it's so good of him to work on Sunday. I don't see how we can stop him."

Then Naomi would sit silent, but not reading, and would presently announce that she had counted the striking of that note twenty-nine times in succession. Once she made it sixty-six; but the piano-tuner behind the closed door had broken his own record, and seemed in a fair way of hammering out the same note a hundred times running, when Monty Gilroy came tramping along the veranda with blinking yellow eyelashes, and his red face pale with temper. Miss Pryse was keeping tally aloud when the manager blundered upon the scene.

"I say, Naomi, how long is this to go on?" exclaimed Gilroy, in a tone that was half-complaining, half-injured, but wholly different from that which he had employed toward her the night before.

"Eighty-three, eighty-four, eighty-five," counted Naomi, giving him a nod and a smile.

"I hadn't been asleep ten minutes when he awoke me with his infernal din."

"Ninety, ninety-one, ninety-two, ninety-three—"

"It's no joke when a man has been over the board the whole week," said Gilroy, trying to smile nevertheless.

"Ninety-seven, ninety-eight—well, I'll be jiggered!"

"Ninety-eight it is," said Tom Chester.

"Yes, he's changed the note. He might have given it a couple more! Still, it's the record. Now, Monty, please forgive us; we're trying to make the best of a bad job, as you see."

"It is a bad job," assented Gilroy, whose rueful countenance concealed (but not from the girl) a vile temper smouldering. "It's pretty rough, I think, on us chaps who've been working like Kanakas all the week."

"Well, but you were pretty rough upon poor Mr. Engelhardt last night; so don't you think that it serves you quite right?"

"Poor Mr. Engelhardt!" echoed Gilroy, savagely. "So it serves us right, does it?" He forced a laugh. "What do you say, Tom?"

"I think it serves you right, too," answered Tom Chester, coolly.

Gilroy laughed again.

"So you're crackin', old chap," said he, genially. He generally was genial with Tom Chester, for whom he entertained a hatred enhanced by fear. "But I say, Naomi, need this sort of thing go on all the afternoon?"

"If it doesn't he will have to stay till to-morrow."

"Ah! I see."

"I thought you would. The piano was in a bad way, and he said there was a long day's work in it; but he seems anxious to get away this evening, that's why he began before breakfast."

"Then let him stick to it, by all means, and we'll all clear out together. I'll see that his horse is run up—I'll go now."

He went.

"That's the most jealous gentleman in this colony," said Naomi to her companion. "He'd rather suffer anything than leave this little piano-tuner and me alone together!"

"Poor little chap," said Chester of the musician; he had nothing to say about Gilroy, who was still in view from the veranda, a swaggering figure in the strong sunlight, with his hands in his cross-cut breeches' pockets, his elbows sticking out, and the strut of a cock on its own midden. Tom Chester watched him with a hard light in his clear eye, and a moistening of the palms of his hands. Tom was pretty good with his fists, and for many a weary month he had been spoiling for a fight with Monty Gilroy, who very likely was not the only jealous gentleman on Taroomba.

All this time the piano-tuner was at his fiendish work behind the closed door, over which Naomi Pryse had purposely mounted guard. Distracting repetitions of one note were varied only by depressing octaves and irritating thirds. Occasionally a chord or two promised a trial trip over the keys, but such promises were never fulfilled. At last Naomi shut her book, with a hopeless smile at Tom Chester, who was ready for her with an answering grin.

"Really, I can't stand it any longer, Mr. Chester."

"You have borne it like a man, Miss Pryse."

"I wanted to make sure that nobody bothered him. Do you think we may safely leave him now?"

"Quite safely. Gilroy is up at the yards, and Sanderson only plays the fool to an audience. Let me pull you out of your chair."

"Thanks. That's it. Let us stroll up to the horse-paddock gate and back; then it will be time for tea; and let's hope our little tuner will have finished his work at last."

"I believe he has finished now," Tom Chester said, as they turned their backs on the homestead. "He's never run up and down the board like that before."

"The board!" said Miss Pryse, laughing. "No, don't you believe it; he won't finish for another hour."

Tom Chester was right, however. As Naomi and he passed out of earshot, the piano-tuner faced about on the music-stool, and peered wistfully through the empty room at the closed door, straining his ear for their voices. Of course he heard nothing; but the talking on the veranda had never been continuous, so that did not surprise him. It gladdened him, rather. She was reading. She might be alone; his heart beat quicker for the thought. She had sat there all day, of her own kind will, enduring his melancholy performance; now she should have her reward. His eyes glistened as he searched in his memory for some restful, dreamy melody, which should at once soothe and charm her ears aching from his crude unmusical monotonies. Suddenly he rubbed his hands, and then stretching them out and leaning backward on the stool he let his fingers fall with their lightest and daintiest touch upon Naomi's old piano.

He had chosen a very simple, well-known piece; but it need not be so well known in the bush. Miss Pryse might never have heard it before, in which case she could not fail to be enchanted. It was the

"Schlummerlied" of Schumann, and the piano-tuner played it with all the very considerable feeling and refinement of which he was capable, and with a smile all the time for its exceeding appropriateness. What could chime more truly with the lazy stillness of the Sunday afternoon than this sweet, bewitching lullaby? Engelhardt had always loved it; but never in his life had he played it half so well. As he finished—softly, but not so softly as to risk a single note dropping short of the veranda—he wheeled round again with a sudden self-conscious movement. It was as though he expected to find the door open and Naomi entranced upon the threshold. It is a fact that he sat watching the door-handle to see it turn, first with eagerness, and at last with acute disappointment. His disappointment was no greater when he opened the door himself and saw the book lying in the empty chair. That, indeed, was a relief. To find her sitting there unmoved was what his soul had dreaded.

But now that his work was done, the piano-tuner felt very lonely and unhappy. To escape from these men with whom he could not get on was his strongest desire but one; the other was to stay and see more of the glorious girl who had befriended him; and he was torn between the two, because his longing for love was scarcely more innate than his shrinking from ridicule and scorn. He knew this, too, and had as profound a scorn for himself as any he was likely to meet with from another. His saving grace was the moral courage which enabled him to run counter to his own craven inclinations.

Thus in the early morning he had apologized to Sanderson, the store-keeper, for the loss of his temper overnight; after lying awake for hours chewing the bitterness of this humiliating move, he had determined upon it in the end. But determination was what he had—it takes not a little to bring you to apologize in cold blood to a rougher man than yourself. Engelhardt had done this, and more. At breakfast and at dinner he had made heroic efforts to be affable and at ease with the men who despised him; though each attempt touched a fresh nerve in his sensitive, self-conscious soul. And now, because from the veranda he could descry Gilroy and Sanderson up at the stock-yards, and because these men were the very two whose society he most dreaded, his will was that he must join them then and there.

He was a man himself; and if he could not get on with other men, that was his own lookout. No doubt, too, it was his own fault. It was a fault of which he swore an oath that he would either cure himself or suffer the consequences like a man. He may even have taken a private pride in being game against the grain. There is no fathoming the thoughts that generate action in egotistical, but noble, natures, whose worst enemy is their own inner consciousness.

Gilroy and Sanderson were in the horse-yard, leaning backward against the heavy white rails. Their pipes were in their mouths, and they were watching Sam Rowntree stalk a wiry bay horse that took some catching. Sam was the groom, and he had just run up all the horses out of the horse-paddock. The yard was full of them. Gilroy hauled a freckled hand out of a cross pocket to point at the piano-tuner's nag.

"Poor-looking devil," said he.

"Yes, the kind you see when you're out without a gun," remarked the wit. "Quite good enough for a thing like him, though." Some association of ideas caused him to glance round toward the homestead through the rails. "By the hokey, here's the thing itself!" he cried.

The pair watched Engelhardt approach.

"I'd like to break his beastly head for him," muttered the manager. "The cheek of him, spoiling our spell with that cursed row!"

The piano-tuner came up with a pleasant smile that was an effort to him, and pretended not to notice Sanderson's stock remark, that "queer things come out after the rain."

"You'll be glad to hear, gentlemen, that I've finished my job," said he, airily.

"Thank God," growled Gilroy.

"I know it's been a great infliction—"

"Oh, no, not at all," said Sanderson, winking desperately. "We liked it. It's just what we do like. You bet!"

The wiry bay horse had been caught by this time, and Sam Rowntree was saddling it, by degrees, for the animal was obviously fresh and touchy. Engelhardt watched the performance with a bitter feeling of envy for all Australian men, and of contempt for himself because they contemned him. The fault was his, not theirs. He was of a different order from these rough, light-hearted men—of an altogether inferior order, as it seemed to his self-criticising mind. But that was no excuse for his not getting on with them, and as a rider puts his horse at a fence again and again, so Engelhardt spurred himself on to one more effort to do so.

"That's your horse, Mr. Gilroy?"

"Yes."

"I saw the 'G' on the left shoulder."

"You mean the near shoulder; a horse hasn't a left."

"No? I'm not well up in horses. What's his name?"

"Hard Times."

"That's good! I like his looks, too—not that I know anything about horses."

Here Sanderson whispered something to Gilroy, who said carelessly to Engelhardt:

"Can you ride?"

"I can ride my own moke."

"Like a turn on Hard Times?"

"Yes! I should."

This was said in a manner that was all the more decided for the moments of deliberation which preceded it. The piano-tuner was paler even than usual, but all at once his jaw had grown hard and strong, and there was a keen light in his eyes. The others looked at him, unable to determine whether it was a good rider they were dealing with or a born fool.

"Fetch him out of the yard, Sam," said Gilroy to the groom. "This gentleman here is going to draw first blood."

Sam Rowntree stared.

"You'd better not, mister," said he, looking doubtfully at the musician. "He's fresh off the grass—hasn't had the saddle on him for two months."

"Get away, Sam. The gentleman means to take some of the cussedness out of him. Isn't that it, Engelhardt?"

"I mean to try," said Engelhardt, quietly.

A lanky middle-aged bushman, who had loafed across from the men's hut, here spat into the sand without removing the pipe from his teeth, and put in his word.

"Becod, then ye're a brave man! He bucks like beggary. He's bucked me as high as a blessed house!"

"We'll see how high he can buck me," said Engelhardt.

Gilroy was losing interest in the proceedings. The little fool could ride after all; instead of being scored off, he was going to score. The manager thrust his hands deep in his cross pockets, and watched sullenly, with his yellow eyelashes drooping over his blue eyes. Suddenly he strode forward, crying:

"What the blazes are you up to, you idiot?"

Engelhardt had shown signs of mounting on the off-side, but was smiling as though he had done it on purpose.

"He's all right," said the long stockman with the pipe. "He knows a thing or two, my word."

But his style of mounting in the end hardly tallied with this theory. The piano-tuner scrambled into the saddle, and kicked about awkwardly before finding his stirrups; and the next thing he did was to job the horse's mouth with the wanton recklessness of pure innocence. The watchers held their breath. As for Hard Times, he seemed to know that he was bestridden by an unworthy foeman, to appreciate the humor of the situation, and to make up his evil mind to treat it humorously as it deserved. Away he went, along the broad road between homestead and yards, at the sweetest and most guileless canter. The rider was sitting awkwardly enough, but evidently as tight as he knew how. And he needed all the grip within the power of his loins and knees. Half-way to the house, without a single premonitory symptom, the wiry bay leapt clean into the air, with all its legs gathered up under its body, its head tucked between its knees, and its back arched like a bent bow. Down it came, with a thud, then up again like a ball, again and again, and yet again.

At the first buck Engelhardt stuck nobly; he evidently had been prepared for the worst. The second displayed a triangle of blue sky between his legs and the saddle; he had lost his stirrups and the reins, but was clinging to the mane with all ten fingers, and to the saddle with knees and shins.

"Sit tight!" roared Gilroy. "Stick to him!" yelled Sanderson. "Slide off as he comes down!" shouted the groom.

But if Engelhardt heard them he did not understand. He only knew that for the first time in his life he was on a buck-jumper, and that he meant to stay there as long as the Lord would let him. A wild exhilaration swamped every other sensation. The blue sky fell before him like a curtain at each buck; at the fifth his body was seen against it like a burst balloon; and after that, Hard Times was left to the more difficult but less exciting task of bucking himself out of an empty saddle.

They carried Engelhardt toward the house. But Naomi came running out and met them half-way, and Tom Chester was at her back. From the veranda the two had seen it happen. And in all that was done during the next minutes Naomi was prime mover.

"You call yourselves men. Men indeed! There's more manhood lying here than ever there was or will be in the two of you put together!"

"Hear, hear!"

The voices were those of Miss Pryse and Tom Chester. They were the first that Engelhardt heard when his senses came back to him. But the first thing that was said to him when he opened his eyes was said by Gilroy:

"Why the devil didn't you tell us you couldn't ride?"

He did not answer, but Tom Chester said coolly before them all:

"He can ride a jolly sight better than you can, Gilroy. You sit five bucks and I'll give you five notes."

There was bad blood in the air. The piano-tuner could not help it. His head was all wrong, and his right arm felt red-hot from wrist to elbow; he discovered that it was bare, and in the hands of Miss Pryse. He felt ashamed, it was such a thin arm. But Miss Pryse smiled at him kindly, and he smiled faintly back at her; he just saw Tom Chester tearing the yellow backs off a novel, and handing them to the kneeling girl; then once more he closed his eyes.

"He's off again," said Naomi. "Thank God I can set a joint. There's nothing to watch, all of you! Sam, you may as well turn out this gentleman's horse again. If anybody thought of getting rid of him to-night, they've gone the wrong way about it, for now he shall stay here till he's able to go on tuning pianos."

And as she spoke Naomi looked up, and sent her manager to the rightabout with a single stare of contempt and defiance.

CHAPTER IV

THE TREASURE IN THE STORE

When Engelhardt regained consciousness he found himself spread out on his bed in the barracks, with Tom Chester rather gingerly pulling off his clothes for him as he lay. The first thing he saw was his own heavily splintered arm stretched stiffly across his chest. For the moment this puzzled him. His mind was slow to own so much lumber as a part of his person. Then he remembered, and let his lids fall back without speaking. His head ached abominably, but it was rapidly clearing, both as to what had happened and what was happening now. With slight, instinctive movements, first of one limb, then another, he immediately lightened Tom Chester's task. Presently he realized that he was between the sheets and on the point of being left to himself. This put some life in him for perhaps the space of a minute.

"Thank you," he said, opening his eyes again. "That was awfully good of you."

"What was?" asked the other, in some astonishment. "I thought you were stunned."

"No, not this last minute or two; but my head's splitting; I want to sleep it off."

"Poor chap! I'll leave you now. But what induced you to tackle Hard Times, when you weren't a rider, sweet Heaven only knows!"

"I was a fool," said Engelhardt, wearily.

"You leave that for us to say," returned the other. "You've got some pluck, whatever you are, and that's about all you want in the bush. So long."

He went straight to Naomi, who was awaiting him outside with considerable anxiety. They hovered near the barracks, talking all things over for some time longer. Then Naomi herself stole with soft, bold steps to the piano-tuner's door. There she hesitated, one hand on the latch, the other at her ear. It ended in her entering his room on tiptoe. A moment later she was back in the yard, her fine face shining with relief.

"He's sleeping like a baby," she said to Chester. "I think we may perhaps make our minds easy about him now—don't you? I was terribly frightened of concussion; but that's all right, or he wouldn't be breathing as he is now. We'll let him be for an hour or two, and then send Mrs. Potter to him with some toast and tea. Perhaps you'll look him up last thing, Mr. Chester, and give him a hand in the morning if he feels well enough to get up?"

"Certainly I would, Miss Pryse, if I were here; but we were all going out to the shed to-night, as usual, so as to make an early start—"

"I know; I know. And very glad I shall be to get quit of the others; but I have this poor young man on my mind, and you at least must stop till morning to see me through. I shall mention it myself to Mr. Gilroy."

"Very well," said Chester, who was only too charmed with the plan. "I'll stop, with all my heart, and be very glad to do anything that I can."

With Chester it was certainly two for himself and one for the unlucky Engelhardt. He made the most of his evening with Naomi all to himself. It was not a very long evening, for Gilroy delayed his departure to the last limit, and then drove off in a sullen fury, spitting oaths right and left and lashing his horses like a madman. This mood of the manager's left Chester in higher spirits than ever; he had the satisfaction of feeling himself partly responsible for it. Moreover, he had given Gilroy, whom he frankly detested, the most excellent provocation to abuse him to his face before starting; but, as usual, the opening had been declined. Such were the manager of Taroomba and his subordinate the overseer; the case was sufficiently characteristic of them both. As for Chester, he made entertaining talk with Naomi as long as she would sit up, and left her with an assurance that he would attend to the piano-tuner like a mother. Nor was he much worse than his word; though the patient knew nothing until awakened next morning by the clatter and jingle of boots and spurs at his bedside.

"What is it?" he cried, struggling to sit up.

"Me," said Chester. "Lie perfectly tight. I only came to tell you that your breakfast's coming in directly, and to see how you are. How are you? Had some sleep?"

"Any quantity," said Engelhardt, with a laugh that slipped into a yawn. "I feel another man."

"How's the arm?"

"I don't feel to have one. I suppose it's broken, is it?"

"No, my boy, only dislocated. So Miss Pryse said when she fixed it up, and she knows all about that sort of thing. How's the head?"

"Right as the bank!"

"I don't believe you. You're the color of candles. If you feel fit to get up, after you've had something to eat, I'm to give you a hand; but if I were you I'd lie in."

"Die first," cried the piano-tuner, laughing heartily with his white face.

"Well, we'll see. Here comes Mother Potter with your breakfast. I'll be back in half an hour, and we'll see about it then."

Chester came back to find the piano-tuner half dressed with his one hand. He was stripped and dripping to the waist, and he raised his head so vigorously from the cold water, at the overseer's entrance, that the latter was well splashed.

"Dry me," he cried.

The overseer did his best.

"I feel as fit as a Strad," panted Engelhardt.

"What may that be?"

"A fiddle and a half."

"Then you don't look it."

"But I soon shall. What's a dislocated arm? Steady on, I say, though. Easy over the stones!"

Chester was nonplussed.

"My dear fellow, you're bruised all over. It'd be cruel to touch you with a towel of cotton-wool."

"Go on," said Engelhardt. "I must be dried and dressed. Dry away! I can stand it."

The other exercised the very greatest care; but ribs and shoulders on the same side as the injured arm were fairly dappled with bruises, and it was perfectly impossible not to hurt. Once he caught Engelhardt wincing. He was busy at his back, and only saw it in the mirror.

"I am hurting you!" he cried.

"Not a bit, sir. Fire away!"

The white face in the mirror was still racked with pain.

"Where did you get your pluck?" asked Chester, casually, when all was over.

"From my mother," was the prompt reply; "such as I possess."

"My boy," said Chester, "you've as much as most!" And, without thinking, he slapped the other only too heartily on the bruised shoulder. Next moment he was sufficiently horrified at what he had done, for this time the pain was more than the sufferer could conceal. In an instant, however, he was laughing off his friend's apologies with no less tact than self-control.

"You're about the pluckiest little devil I've ever seen," said the overseer at last. "I thought so yesterday— I know so to-day."

The piano-tuner beamed with joy. "What rot," however, was all he said.

"Not it, my boy! You're a good sort. You've got as much pluck in one hair of your head—though they are long 'uns, mind—as that fellow Gilroy has in his whole composition. Now I must be off to the shed. I should stroll about in the air, if I were you, but keep out of the sun. If you care to smoke, you'll find a tin of cut-up on the corner bracket in my room, and Miss Pryse'll give you a new pipe out of the store if you want one. You'll see her about pretty soon, I should say. Oh, yes, she had breakfast with me. She means to keep you by main force till you're up to piano-tuning again. Serve Gilroy jolly well right, the brute! So we'll meet again this week-end; meanwhile, good-by, old chap, and more power to the arm."

Engelhardt watched the overseer out of sight, with a mingled warmth and lightness of heart which for the moment were making an unusually happy young man of him. This Chester was the very incarnation of a type that commonly treated him, as he was too ready to fancy, with contempt; and yet that was the type of all others whose friendship and admiration he coveted most. All his life he had been so shy and so sensitive that the good in him, the very best of him, was an unknown quantity to all save those who by accident or intimacy struck home to his inner nature. The latter was true as steel, and brave, patient, and enduring to an unsuspected degree; but a cluster of small faults hid this from the ordinary eye. The man was a little too anxious to please—to do the right thing—to be liked or loved by those with whom he mixed. As a natural consequence, his anxiety defeated his design. Again, he was a little too apt to be either proud or ashamed of himself—one or the other—he never could let himself alone. Wherefore appreciation was inordinately sweet to his soul, and the reverse proportionately bitter. Mere indifference hurt him no less than active disdain; indeed, where there was the former, he was in the bad habit of supposing the latter; and thus the normal current of his life was never clear of little unnecessary griefs of which he was ashamed to speak, but which he only magnified by keeping them to himself. Perhaps he had his compensating joys. Certainly he was as often in exceedingly high spirits as in the dumps, and it is just possible that the former are worth the latter. In any case he was in the best of spirits this morning; nor by any means ashamed of his slung arm, but rather the reverse, if the whole truth be told. And yet, with a fine girl like Naomi, and a smart bushman like Tom Chester, both thinking well of him together, there surely was for once some slight excuse for an attack of self-satisfaction. It was transitory enough, and rare enough, too, Heaven knows.

In this humor, at all events, he wandered about the yard for some time, watching the veranda incessantly with jealous eyes. His saunterings led him past the rather elaborate well, in the centre of the open space, to the store on the farther side. This was a solid isolated building, very strongly built, with an outer coating of cement, and a corrugated roof broken on the foremost slope by a large-sized skylight. A shallow veranda ran in front, but was neither continued at the ends nor renewed at the back of the building. Nor were there any windows; the piano-tuner walked right round to see, and on coming back to the door (a remarkably strong one) there was Naomi fitting in her key. She was wearing an old black dress, an obvious item of her cast-off mourning, and over it, from her bosom to her toes, a brilliantly white apron, which struck Engelhardt as the most charming garment he had ever seen.

"Good business!" she cried at sight of him. "I know how you are from Mr. Chester. Just hold these things while I take both hands to this key; it always is so stiff."

The things in question, which she reached out to him with her left hand, consisted of a box of plate-powder, a piece of chamois leather, a tooth-brush, and a small bottle of methylated spirits; the lot lying huddled together in a saucer.

"That does it," continued Naomi as the lock shot back with a bang and the door flew open. "Now come on in. You can lend me your only hand. I never thought of that."

Engelhardt followed her into the store. Inside it was one big room, filled with a good but subdued light (for as yet the sun was beating upon the hinder slope of corrugated iron), and with those motley necessaries of station life which are to be seen in every station store. Sides of bacon, empty ration-bags, horse-collars and hames, bridles and reins, hung promiscuously from the beams. Australian saddles kept their balance on stout pegs jutting out from the walls. The latter were barely lined with shelves, like book-cases, but laden with tinned provisions of every possible description, sauces and patent medicines in bottles, whiskey and ink in stone jars, cases of tea, tobacco, raisins, and figs. Engelhardt noticed a great green safe, with a couple of shot-guns and a repeating-rifle in a rack beside it, and two or three pairs of rusty hand-cuffs on a nail hard by. The floor was fairly open, but for a few sacks of flour in a far corner. It was cut up, however, by a raised desk with a high office-stool to it, and by the permanent, solid-looking counter which faced the door. A pair of scales, of considerable size and capacity, was the one encumbrance on the counter. Naomi at once proceeded to remove it, first tossing the weights onto the flour bags, one after the other, and then lifting down the scales before Engelhardt had time to help her. Thereafter she slapped the counter with her flat hand, and stood looking quizzically at her guest.

"You don't know what's under this counter," she said at last, announcing an obvious fact with extraordinary unction.

"I don't, indeed," said the piano-tuner, shaking his head.

"Nor does your friend Mr. Sanderson, though he's the store-keeper. He's out at the shed during shearing-time, branding bales and seeing to the loading of the drays. But all the rest of the year he keeps the books at that desk or serves out rations across this counter; and yet he little dreams what's underneath it."

"You interest me immensely, Miss Pryse."

"I wonder if I dare interest you any more?"

"You had better not trust me with a secret."

"Why not? Do you mean that you couldn't keep one?"

"I don't say that; but I have no right—"

"Right be bothered," cried Naomi, crisply; "there's no question of right."

Engelhardt colored up.

"I was only going to say that I had no right to get in your way and perhaps make you feel it was better to tell me things than to turn me out," he explained, humbly. "I shall turn myself out, since you are too kind to do it for me. I meant in any case to take a walk in the pines."

"Did I invite you to come in here, or did I not?" inquired Miss Pryse.

"Well, only to carry these things. Here they are."

He held them out to her, but she refused to look at them.

"When I tell you I don't want you, then it will be time for you to go," she said. "Since you don't live here, there's not the least reason why you shouldn't know what no man on the place knows, except Mr. Gilroy. Besides, you can really help me. So now will you be good?"

"I'll try," said Engelhardt, catching her smile.

"Then I forgive everything. Now listen to me. My dear father was the best and kindest man in all the world; but he had his fair share of eccentricity. I have mine, too; and you most certainly have yours; but that's neither here nor there. My father came of a pretty good old Welsh family. In case you think I'm swaggering about it, let me tell you I'd like to take that family and drop the whole crew in the well outside—yes, and heat up the water to boil 'em before they'd time to drown! I owe them nothing nice, don't you believe it. They treated my father shamefully; but he was the eldest son, and when the old savage, his father, had the good taste to die, mine went home and collared his dues. He didn't get much beyond the family plate; but sure enough he came back with that. And didn't the family sit up, that's all!

However, his eccentricity came in then. He must needs bring that plate up here. It's here still. I'm sitting on it now!"

Indeed, she had perched herself on the counter while speaking; and now, spinning round where she sat, she was down on the other side and fumbling at a padlock before her companion could open his mouth.

"Isn't it very dangerous?" he said at length, as Naomi stood up and set the padlock on the desk.

"Hardly that. Mr. Gilroy is absolutely the only person who knows that it is here. Still, the bank would be best, of course, and I mean to have it all taken there one of these days. Meanwhile, I clean my silver whenever I come up here. It's a splendid opportunity when my young men are all out at the shed. I did a lot last week, and I expect to finish off this morning."

As she spoke the top of the counter answered to the effort of her two strong arms, and came up with a jerk. She raised it until it caught, when Engelhardt could just get his chin over the rim, and see a huge, heavily clamped plate-chest lying like a kernel in its shell. There were more locks to undo. Then the baize-lined lid of the chest was raised in its turn. And in a very few minutes the Taroomba store presented a scene which it would have been more than difficult to match throughout the length and breadth of the Australian bush.

CHAPTER V

MASTERLESS MEN

Naomi had seated herself on the tall stool at the bookkeeper's desk, on which she had placed in array the silver that was still unclean. This included a fine old epergne, of quaint design and exceedingly solid proportions; a pair of candlesticks, in the familiar form of the Corinthian column—more modern, but equally handsome in their way; a silver coffee-pot with an ivory handle; and a number of ancient skewers. She tackled the candlesticks first. They were less tarnished than might have been expected, and in Naomi's energetic hands they soon regained their pristine purity and lustre. As she worked she talked freely of her father, and his family in Wales, to Engelhardt, for whose benefit she had unpacked many of the things which she had already cleaned, and set them out upon the counter after shutting it down as before. He, too, was seated, on the counter's farther edge, with his back half-turned to the door. And the revelation of so much treasure in that wild place made him more and more uneasy.

"I should have thought you'd be frightened to have this sort of thing on the premises," he could not help saying.

"Frightened of what?"

"Well—bushrangers."

"They don't exist. They're as extinct as the dodo. But that reminds me!"

She broke off abruptly, and sat staring thoughtfully at the door, which was standing ajar. She even gave the steps of her Corinthian column a rest from tooth-brush and plate-powder.

"That reminds you?"

"Yes—of bushrangers. We once had some here, before they became extinct."

"Since you've had the plate?"

"Yes; it was the plate they were after. How they got wind of it no one ever knew."

"Is it many years ago?"

"Well, I was quite a little girl at the time. But I never shall forget it! I woke in the night, hearing shots, and I ran into the veranda in my night-dress. There was my father behind one of the veranda posts, with a revolver in each hand, roaring and laughing as though it were the greatest joke in the world; and there were two men in the store veranda, just outside this door. They were shooting at father, all they knew, but they couldn't hit him, though they hit the post nearly every time. I'll show you the marks when we go over to lunch. My father kept laughing and shooting at them the whole time. It was just the sort of game he liked. But at last one of the men fell in a heap outside the door, and then the other bolted for his horse. He got away, too; but he left something behind him that he'll never replace in this world or the next."

"What was that?" asked Engelhardt with a long breath.

"His little finger. My father amputated it with one of his shots. It was picked up between this and the place where he mounted his horse. Father got him on the wing!" said Naomi, proudly.

"Was he caught?"

"No, he was never heard of again."

"And the man who was shot?"

"He was as dead as sardines. And who do you suppose he turned out to be?"

Engelhardt shook his head.

"Tigerskin the bushranger! No less! It was a dirty burgling business for a decent bushranger to lose his life in, now wasn't it? For they never stuck up the station, mind you; they were caught trying to burst into the store. Luckily, they didn't succeed. The best of it was that at the inquest, and all that, it never came out what it was they really wanted in our store. Soon afterward my father had the windows blocked up and the whole place cemented over, as you see it now."

Naomi was done. Back went the tooth-brush to work on the Corinthian column, and Engelhardt saw more of the pretty hair, but less of the sweet face, as she bent to her task with redoubled vigor. Sweet she most certainly was in his sight, and yet she could sit there, and tell him of blood spilt and life lost before her own soft eyes, as calmly as though such sights were a natural part of a young girl's education. For a space he so marvelled at her that there was room in his soul for no other sensation. Then the towering sun struck down through the skylight, setting light to the silver, and brushing the girl's hair as she leant forward, so that it shone like spun copper. From that moment the piano-tuner could only and slavishly admire; but he was not allowed much time for this slightly perilous recreation. Abruptly, impulsively, as she did most things, Naomi raised her face and gave him a nod.

"Now, Mr. Engelhardt, it's your turn to talk. I've done my share. Who are you, where do you come from, and what's your ambition in life? It really is time I knew something more about you."

The poor fellow was so taken aback, and showed it so plainly, that Naomi simplified her question without loss of time.

"It doesn't matter who you are, since you're a very nice young man—which is the main thing. And I know that you hail from old England, which is all I have any business to know. But come! you must have some ambitions. I like all young men to have their ambitions. I distrust them when they have none. So what's yours? Out with it quick!"

She discerned delight behind his blushes.

"Come on, I can't wait! What is it?"

"I suppose it's music."

"I knew it. Oh, but that's such a splendid ambition!"

"Do you really think so?"

"It's grand! But what do you aspire to do? Mephistopheles or Faust in the opera? Or sentimental songs in your dress-suit, with a tea-rose in your button-hole and a signet-ring plain as a pike-staff to the back row? Somehow or other I don't think you're sleek enough for a tenor or coarse enough for a bass. Certainly I know nothing at all about it."

"Oh, Miss Pryse, I can't sing a bit!"

"My dear young man, I've heard you."

"I only tried because they made me—and to sell my wretched songs."

"Then is it to be solos on the piano?"

"I'm not good enough to earn my rations at that."

"The organ—and a monkey? Burnt cork and the bones?"

"Oh, Miss Pryse!"

"Well, then, what?"

"How can I say it? I should like, above everything else—if only I ever could!—to write music—to compose." He said it shyly enough, with downcast eyes, and more of his blushes.

"And why not?"

"Well, I don't know why not—one of these days."

His tone had changed. He had tossed up his head erect. She had not laughed at him after all!

"I should say that you would compose very well indeed," remarked Naomi, naïvely.

"I don't know that; but some day or other I mean to try."

"Then why waste your time tuning pianos?"

"To keep myself alive meanwhile. I don't say that I shall ever do any good as a composer. Only that's what you'd call my ambition. In any case, I don't know enough to try yet, except to amuse myself when I'm alone. I have no technique. I know only the rudiments of harmony. I do get ideas; but they're no use to me. I haven't enough knowledge—of treatment—of composition—to turn them to any account. But I shall have some day! Miss Pryse, do you know why I'm out here? To make enough money to go back again and study—and learn my trade—with plenty of time and pains—which all trades require and demand. I mean all artistic trades. And I'm not doing so very badly, seeing I've only been out three years. I really am beginning to make a little. It was my mother's idea, my coming out at all. I wasn't twenty-three at the time. It was a splendid idea, like everything she does or says or thinks! How I wish you knew my mother! She is the best and cleverest woman in all the world, though she is so poor, and has lived in a cottage all her life. My father was a German. He was clever, too, but he wasn't practical. So he never succeeded. But my mother is everything! One day I shall go back to her with my little pile. Then we shall go abroad together—perhaps to Milan—and I shall study hard-all, and we'll soon find out whether there's anything in me or not. If there isn't, back I come to the colonies to tune pianos and sell music; but my mother shall come with me next time."

"You will find that there is something in you," said Naomi. "I can see it."

Indeed, it was not unreasonable to suppose that there was something behind that broad, high forehead and those enthusiastic and yet intelligent eyes. The mouth, too, was the delicate, mobile mouth of the born artist; the nostrils were as sensitive as those of a thoroughbred racehorse; and as he spoke the young man's face went white-hot with sheer enthusiasm. Clearly there was reason in what Naomi thought and said, though she knew little about music and cared less. He beamed at her without answering, and she spoke again.

"Certainly you have ambition," she said; "and honestly, there's nothing I admire so much in a young man. Please understand that I for one am with you heart and soul in all you undertake or attempt. I feel quite sure that I shall live to see you famous. Oh, isn't it splendid to be a man and aim so high?"

"It is," he answered, simply, out of the frankness of his heart.

"Even if you never succeed, it is fine to try!"

"Thank Heaven for that. Even if you never succeed!"

"But you are going to—"

"Or going to know the reason why!"

To a sympathetic young woman who believes in him, and thus stimulates his belief in himself; who is ready with a nod and a smile when his mind outstrips his tongue; who understands his incoherences, and is with him in his wildest nights; to such a listener the ordinary young man with enthusiasm can talk by the hour together, and does. Naomi was one such; she was eminently understanding. Engelhardt had enthusiasm. He had more than it is good for a man to carry about in his own breast. And there is no doubt that he would have spent the entire morning in putting his burden, bit by bit, upon Naomi as she sat and worked and listened, had no interruption occurred. As it was, however, she interrupted him herself, and that in the middle of a fresh tirade, by suddenly holding up her finger and sharply enjoining silence.

"Don't you hear voices?" she said.

He listened.

"Yes, I do."

"Do you mind seeing who it is?"

He went to the door. "There are two men hanging about the station veranda," he said. "Stay! Now they have seen me, and are coming this way."

Naomi said not one word, but she managed to fetch over the office-stool in the haste with which she sprang to the ground. At a run she rounded the counter, and reached the door just as the men came up. She pushed Engelhardt out first, and then followed him herself, locking the door and putting the key in her pocket before turning to the men. Last of all, but in her most amiable manner, she asked them what they wanted.

"Travellers' rations," said one.

"Especially meat," added the other.

"Very good," said Naomi, "go to the kitchen and get the meat first. Mr. Engelhardt, you may not know the station custom of giving rations to travellers. We don't give meat here as a rule; so will you take these men over to the kitchen, and tell Mrs. Potter I wish them each to have a good helping of cold mutton? Then bring them back to the store."

"We don't seek no favors," growled the man who had spoken first.

"No?" said Naomi, with a charming smile. "But I'm sure you need some meat. What's more, I mean you to have some!"

"Suppose we take the tea and flour first, now we are at the store!"

"Ah, I can't attend to you for a few minutes," said the girl, casually. As she spoke she turned and left them, and Engelhardt gathered her unconcern from the snatch of a song as she entered the main building. The men accompanied him to the kitchen in a moody silence. As for himself, he already felt an extraordinary aversion for them both.

And indeed their looks were against them. The one who had spoken offensively about the meat was a stout, thick-set, middle-aged man, who gave an impression of considerable activity in spite of his great girth. Half his face was covered with short gray bristles, like steel spikes. Though his hands were never out of his pockets, he carried his head like a man of character; but the full force of a bold, insolent, vindictive expression was split and spoilt by the most villanous of squints. Nevertheless the force was there. It was not so conspicuous in his companion, who was, however, almost equally untoward-looking in his own way. He was of the medium size, all bone and gristle like a hawk, and with no sign upon his skin of a drop of red blood underneath. The hands were brown and furry as an ape's, with the nails all crooked and broken by hard work. The face was as brown, and very weather-beaten, with a pair of small black eyes twinkling out of the ruts and puckers like pools in the sun upon a muddy road. This one rolled as he walked, and wore brass rings in his ears; and Engelhardt, who had come out from England in a sailing ship, saw in a moment that he was as salt as junk all through. Decidedly he was the best of the two, though his eyes were never still, nor the hang of his head free and honest. And on the whole the piano-tuner was thankful when his share of the trouble with these men was at an end, and they all came back to the store.

Rather to his surprise, Naomi was there before them, and busy weighing out the traveller's quantum of sugar, tea, and flour, for each man. What was really amazing, however, was the apparent miracle that had put every trace of the silver out of sight.

"No work for us on the station?" said the stout man, before they finally sheered off, and in a tone far from civil, to Engelhardt's thinking.

"None, I'm afraid," said Naomi, again with a smile.

"Nor yet at the shed?" inquired the other, civilly enough.

"Nor yet at the shed, I am sorry to say."

"So long, then," said the fat man, in his impudent manner. "Mayhap we shall be coming to see you again, miss, one o' these fine days or nights. My dear, you look out for us! You keep your spare-room in readiness! A feather-bed for me—"

"Stow it, mate," said the other tramp, as he hitched his swag across his shoulders. "Can't you hump your bluey and come away decent?"

"If you don't," cried Engelhardt, putting in his little word in a gigantic voice, "it will be the worse for you!"

The big fellow laughed and swore.

"Will it, my little man?" said he. "Are you going to make it the worse? I've a blessed good mind to take and crumple you up for manure, I have. And a blessed bad barrerful you'd make! See here, my son, I reckon you've got one broke bone about you already; mind out that I don't leave a few pals to keep it company. A bit more of your cheek, and I'll make you so as your own sweetheart—a fine girl she is, as ought to be above the likes of you; but I suppose you're better than nothing—I tell you I'll make you so as your sweetheart—"

It was the man's own mate who put a stop to this.

"Can't you shut it and come on?" he cried, with a kind of half-amused anger. "Wot good is this going to do either me or you, or any blessed body else?"

"It'll do somebody some harm," returned the other, "if he opens his mouth again. Yes, I'll clear out before I smash 'im! Good-by, my dear, and a bigger size to you in sweethearts. So long, little man. You may thank your broke arm that your 'ead's not broke as well!"

They were gone at last. Naomi and Engelhardt watched them out of sight from the veranda, the latter heaving with rage and indignation. He was not one to forget this degradation in a hurry. Naomi, on the other hand, who had more to complain of, being a woman, was in her usual spirits in five minutes. She took him by the arm, and told him to cheer up. He made bitter answer that he could never forgive himself for having stood by and heard her spoken to as she had been spoken to that morning. She pointed to his useless arm, and laughed heartily.

"As long as they didn't see the silver," said she, "I care very little what they said."

"But I care!"

"Then you are not to. Do you think they saw the silver?"

"No; I'm pretty sure they didn't. How quickly you must have bundled it in again!"

"There was occasion for quickness. We must put it to rights after lunch. Meanwhile come along and look here."

She had led the way along the veranda, and now stood fingering one of the whitewashed posts. It was pocked about the middle with ancient bullet-marks.

"This was the post my father stood behind. Not much of a shelter, was it?"

Engelhardt seemed interested and yet distrait. He made no answer.

"Why don't you speak?" cried Naomi. "What has struck you?"

"Nothing much," he replied. "Only when you heard the voices, and I went to the door, the big brute was showing the little brute this very veranda-post!"

Naomi considered.

"There's not much in that," she said at last. "It's the custom for travellers to wait about a veranda; and what more natural than their spotting these holes and having a look at them? As long as they didn't spot my silver! Do you know why I came over to the house before putting it away?"

"No."

"To get this," said Naomi, pulling something from her pocket. She was laughing rather shyly. It was a small revolver.

CHAPTER VI

£500

"And what is your other name, Mr. Engelhardt?"

"Hermann."

"Hermann Engelhardt! That's a lovely name. How well it will look in the newspapers!"

The piano-tuner shook his head.

"It will never get into them now," said he, sadly.

"What nonsense!" exclaimed the girl. "When you have told me of all the big things you dream of doing one day! You'll do them every one when you go home to England again; I'll put my bottom dollar on you."

"Ah, but the point is whether I shall ever go back at all."

"Of course you will."

"I have a presentiment that I never shall."

"Since when?" inquired Naomi, with a kindly sarcasm.

"Oh, I always have it, more or less."

"You had it very much less this morning, when you were telling me how you'd go home and study at Milan and I don't know where-all, once you'd made the money."

"But I don't suppose I ever shall make it."

"Bless the man!" cried Naomi, giving him up, for the moment in despair. She continued to gaze at him, however, as he leant back in his wicker chair, with hopeless dark eyes fixed absently upon the distant clumps of pale green trees that came between glaring plain and cloudless sky. They were sitting on the veranda which did not face the station-yard, because it was the shady one in the afternoon. The silver had all been properly put away, and locked up as carefully as before. As for the morning's visitors, Naomi was herself disposed to think no more of them or their impudence; it is therefore sad to relate that her present companion would allow her to forget neither. With him the incident rankled characteristically; it had left him solely occupied by an extravagantly poor opinion of himself. For the time being, this discolored his entire existence and prospects, draining his self-confidence to the last drop. Accordingly, he harped upon the late annoyance, and his own inglorious share in it, to an extent which in another would have tried Naomi very sorely indeed; but in him she rather liked it. She had a book in her lap, but it did not interest her nearly so much as the human volume in the wicker chair at her side. She was exceedingly frank about the matter.

"You're the most interesting man I ever met in my life," was her very next remark.

"I can't think that!"

He had hauled in his eyes some miles to see whether she meant it.

"Nevertheless, it's the case. Do you know why you're so interesting?"

"No, that I don't!"

"Because you're never the same for two seconds together."

His face fell.

"Among other reasons," added Naomi, nodding kindly.

But Engelhardt had promptly put himself upon the spit. He was always doing this.

"Yes, I know I'm a terribly up-and-down kind of chap," said he, miserably; "there's no happy medium about me."

"When you are good you are very good indeed, and when you are bad you are horrid! That's just what I like. I can't stand your always-the-same people. They bore me beyond words; they drill me through and through! Still, you were very good indeed this morning, you know. It is too absurd of you to give a second thought to a couple of tramps and their insolence!"

"I can't help it. I'm built that way. To think that I should have stood still to hear you insulted like that!"

"But you didn't stand still."

"Oh, yes, I did."

"Well, I wish you wouldn't bother about it. I wish you wouldn't bother about yourself."

"When I am bad I am horrid," he said, with a wry smile, "and that's now."

"No, I tell you I like it. I never know where I've got you. That's one reason why you're so interesting."

His face glowed, and he clasped her with his glance.

"How kind you are!" he said, softly. "How you make the best of one, even at one's worst! But oh, how bitterly you make me wish that I were different!"

"I'm very glad that you're not," said Naomi; "everybody else is different."

"But I would give my head to be like everybody else—to be hail-fellow with those men out at the shed, for instance. They wouldn't have stood still this morning."

"Wouldn't you as soon be hail-fellow with me?" asked the girl, ignoring his last sentence.

"A million times sooner, of course! But surely you understand?"

"I think I do."

"I know you do; you understand everything. I never knew anyone like you, never!"

"Then we're quits," said Naomi, as though the game were over. And she closed her eyes. But it was she who began it again; it always was.

"You have one great fault," she said, maternally.

"I have a thousand and one."

"There you are. You think too much about them. You take too much notice of yourself; that's your great fault."

"Yet I didn't think I was conceited."

"Not half enough. That's just it. Yet you are egotistical."

He looked terribly crestfallen. "I suppose I am," he said, dolefully. "In fact, I am."

"Then you're not, so there!"

"Which do you mean?"

"I only said it to tease you. Do you suppose I'd have said such a thing if I'd really thought it?"

"I shouldn't mind what you said. If you really do think me egotistical, pray say so frankly."

"Of course I don't think anything of the kind!"

"Is that the truth?"

"The real truth."

(It was not.)

"If it's egotistical to think absolutely nothing of yourself," continued Naomi, "and to blame yourself and not other people for every little thing that goes wrong, then I should call you a twenty-two-carat egotist. But even then your aims and ambitions would be rather lofty for the billet."

"They never seemed so to me," he whispered, "until you sympathized with them."

"Of course I sympathize," said Naomi, laughing at him. It was necessary to laugh at him now and then. It kept him on his feet; this time it led him from the abstract to the concrete.

"If only I could make enough money to go home and study, to study even in London for one year," murmured Engelhardt, as his eyes drifted out across the plains. "Then I should know whether my dreams ever were worth dreaming. But I have taken root out here, I am beginning to do well, better than ever I could have hoped. At our village in the old country I was glad enough to play the organ in church for twelve pounds a year. Down in Victoria they gave me fifty without a murmur, and I made a little more out of teaching. Oh! didn't I tell you I started life out here as an organist? That's how it was I was able to buy this business, and I am doing very well indeed. Two pounds for tuning a piano! They wouldn't credit it in the old country."

"The man before you used to charge three. A piano-tuner in the bush is an immensely welcome visitor, mind. I don't think I should have lowered my terms at all, especially when you have no intention of doing this sort of thing all your days."

"Ah, well, I shall never dare to throw it up."

"Never's not a word I like to hear you use, Mr. Engelhardt. Remember that you've only been out here three years, and that you are not yet twenty-six. You told me so yourself this morning."

"It's perfectly true," said Engelhardt. "But there's one's mother to consider. I told you about her. I am beginning to send her so much money now. It would be frightful to give that up, just because there are tunes in my head now and then, and I can't put them together in proper harmony."

"I should say that your mother would rather have you than your money, Mr. Engelhardt."

"Perhaps so, but not if I were on her hands composing things that nobody would publish."

"That couldn't be. You would succeed. Something tells me that you would. I see it in your face; I did this morning. I know nothing about music, yet I feel so certain about you. The very fact that you should have these ambitions when you are beginning to do well out here, that in itself is enough for me."

He shook his head, without turning it to thank her by so much as a look. The girl was glad of that. Though he had so little confidence in himself, she knew that the dreams of which he had spoken more freely and more hopefully in the morning were thick upon him then, as he sat in the wicker chair and looked out over the plains, with parted lips and such wistful eyes that Naomi's mind went to work at the promptings of the heart in her which he touched. It was a nimble, practical mind, and the warm heart beneath it was the home of noble impulses, which broke forth continually in kind words and generous acts. Naomi wore that heart upon her sweet frank face, it shone with a clear light out of the fearless eyes that were fixed now so long and so steadily upon the piano-tuner's eager profile. She watched him while the shadow of the building grew broader and broader under his eyes, until all at once it lost its edges, and there were no more sunlit patches on the plain. Still he neither moved nor looked at her. At last she touched him on the arm. She was sitting on his right, and she laid her fingers lightly upon the splints and bandages which were her own handiwork.

"Well, Mr. Engelhardt?"

He started round, and she was smiling at him in the gloaming, with her sweet warm face closer to his than it had ever been before.

"I have been very rude," he stammered.

"I am going to be much ruder."

"Now you are laughing at me."

"No, I am not. I was never farther from laughing in my life, for I fear that I shall offend you, though I do hope not."

He saw that something was upon her mind.

"You couldn't do it if you tried," he said, simply.

"Then I want to know how much money you think you ought to have to go home to England with a clear conscience, and to give yourself heart and soul to music for a year certain? I am so inquisitive about it all."

She was employing, indeed, and successfully, a tone of pure and indefensible curiosity. He thought for some moments before answering. Then he said, quite innocently:

"Five hundred pounds. That would leave me enough to come back and start all over again out here if I failed. I wouldn't tackle it on less."

"But you wouldn't fail. I know nothing about it, but I have my instincts, and I see success in your face. I see it there! And I want to bet on you. I have more money than is good for any girl, and I want to back you for five hundred pounds."

"It is very kind of you," he said, "but you would lose your money." He did not see her meaning. The southern night had set in all at once; he could not even see her strenuous eyes.

"How dense you are," she said, softly, and with a little nervous laugh. "Can't you see that I want to lend you the money?"

"To lend it to me!"

"Why not?"

"Five hundred pounds!"

"My dear young man, I'm ashamed to say that I should never feel it. It's a sporting offer merely. Of course I'd charge interest—you'd dedicate all your nice songs to me. Why don't you answer? I don't like to see you in the bush, it isn't at all the place for you; and I do want to send you home to your mother. You might let me, for her sake. Have you lost your tongue?"

Her hand had remained upon the splints and bandages; indeed, she had forgotten that there was a living arm inside them, but now something trivial occurred that made her withdraw it, and also get up from her chair.

"Are you on, or are you not?"

"Oh, how can I thank you? What can I say?"

"Yes or no," replied Naomi, promptly.

"No, then. I can't—I can't—"

"Then don't. Now not another word! No, there's no offence on either side, unless it's I that have offended you. It was great cheek of me, after all. Yes, it was! Well, then, if it wasn't, will you have the goodness to lend me your ears on an entirely different matter?"

"Very well; with all my heart; yet if only I could ever thank you—"

"If only you would be quiet and listen to me! How are the bruises behaving? That's all I want to hear now."

"The bruises? Oh, they're all right; I'd quite forgotten I had any."

"You can lean back without hurting?"

"Rather! If I put my weight on the left side it doesn't hurt a bit."

"Think you could stand seven miles in a buggy to-morrow morning?"

"Couldn't I!"

"Then I thought of driving over to the shed in the morning; and you shall come with me if you're good."

For an instant he looked radiant. Then his face clouded over as he thought again of her goodness and his own ingratitude.

"Miss Pryse," he began—and stuck—but his tone spoke volumes of remorse and self-abasement.

Evidently she was getting to know that tone, for she caught him up with a look of distinct displeasure.

"Only if you're good, mind!" she told him, sharply. "Not on any account unless!"

And Engelhardt said no more.

CHAPTER VII

THE RINGER OF THE SHED

A sweet breeze and a flawless sky rendered it an exquisite morning when Naomi and her piano-tuner took their seats behind the kind of pair which the girl loved best to handle. They were youngsters both, the one a filly as fresh as paint, the other a chestnut colt, better broken, perhaps, but sufficiently ready to be led astray. The very start was lively. Engelhardt found himself holding on with his only hand as if his life depended on it, instead of on the firm gloved fingers and the taut white-sleeved arm at his side. He looked from the pair of young ones to that arm and those fingers, and back again at the pair. They were pulling alarmingly, especially the filly. Engelhardt took an anxious look at the driver's face. He was prepared to find it resolute but pale. He found it transfigured with the purest exultation. After all, this was the daughter of the man who had returned the bushranger's fire with laughter as loud as his shots; she was her father's child; and from this moment onward the piano-tuner felt it a new honor to be sitting at her side.

"How do you like it?" she found time to ask him when the worst seemed over.

"First-rate," he replied.

"Not in a funk?"

"Not with you."

"That's a blessing. The filly needs watching—little demon! But she sha'n't smash your other arm for you, Mr. Engelhardt, if I can prevent it. No screws loose, Sam, I hope?"

"Not if I knows it, miss!"

Sam Rowntree had jumped on behind to come as far as the first gate, to open it. Already they were there, and as Sam ran in front of the impatient pair the filly shied violently at a blue silk fly-veil which fluttered from his wide-awake.

"That nice youth is the dandy of the men's hut," explained Naomi, as they tore through the gates, leaving Sam and his fly-veil astern in a twinkling. "I daren't say much to him, because he's the only man the hut contains just at present. The rest spend most nights out at the shed, so I should be pretty badly off if I offended Sam. I wasn't too pleased with the state of the buggy, as a matter of fact. It's the old Shanghai my father used to fancy, and somehow it's fallen on idle days; but it runs lighter than anything else we've got, and it's sweetly swung. That's why I chose it for this little trip of ours. You'll find it like a feather-bed for your bruises and bones and things—if only Sam Rowntree used his screw-hammer properly. Feeling happy so far?"

Engelhardt declared that he had never been happier in his life. There was more truth in the assertion than Naomi suspected. She also was happy, but in a different way. A tight rein, an aching arm, a clear course across a five-mile paddock, and her beloved Riverina breeze between her teeth, would have made her happy at any time and in any circumstances. The piano-tuner's company added no sensible zest to a performance which she thoroughly enjoyed for its own sake; but with him the exact opposite was the case. She was not thinking of him. He was thinking only of her. She had her young bloods to watch. His eyes spent half their time upon her grand strong hand and arm. Suddenly these gave a tug and a jerk, both together. But he was in too deep a dream either to see what was wrong or to understand his companion's exclamation.

"He didn't!" she had cried.

"Didn't what?" said Engelhardt. "And who, Miss Pryse?"

"Sam Rowntree didn't use his screw-hammer properly. Wretch! The near swingle-tree's down and trailing."

It took Engelhardt some moments to grasp exactly what she meant. Then he saw. The near swingle-tree was bumping along the ground at the filly's heels, dragged by the traces. Already the filly had shown herself the one to shy as well as to pull, and it now appeared highly probable that she would give a further exhibition of her powers by kicking the Shanghai to matchwood. Luckily, the present pace was too fast for that. The filly had set the pace herself. The filly was keeping it up. As for the chestnut, it was contentedly playing second fiddle with traces drooping like festoons. Thus the buggy was practically being drawn by a single rein with the filly's mouth at one end of it and Naomi's hand at the other.

"Once let the bar tickle her hoofs, and she'll hack us to smithereens," said the latter, cheerfully. "We'll euchre her yet by keeping this up!" And she took her whip and flogged the chestnut.

But this did not ease the strain on her left hand and arm, for the chestnut's pace was nothing to the filly's, so that even with the will he had not the power to tighten his traces and perform his part. Engelhardt saw the veins swelling in the section of wrist between the white sleeve and the dogskin glove. He reached across and tried to help her with his left hand; but she bade him sit quiet, or he would certainly tumble out and be run over; and with her command she sent a roar of laughter into his ear, though the veins were swelling on her forehead, too. Truly she was a chip of the old block, and the grain was as good as ever.

It came to an end at last.

"Hurray!" said Naomi. "I see the fence."

Engelhardt saw it soon after, and in another minute the horses stood smoking, and the buggy panting on its delicate springs, before a six-bar gate which even the filly was disinclined to tackle just then.

"Do you think you can drive through with your one hand, and hold them tight on t'other side?" said Naomi. "Clap your foot on the break and try."

He nodded and managed creditably; but before opening the gate Naomi made a temporary fixture of the swingle-tree by means of a strap; and this proved the last of their troubles. The shed was now plainly in sight, with its long regular roof, and at one end three huts parallel with it and with each other. To the left of the shed, as they drove up, Naomi pointed out the drafting yards. A dense yellow cloud overhung them like a lump of London fog.

"They're drafting now," said Naomi. "I expect Mr. Gilroy is drafting himself. If so, let's hope he's too busy to see us. It would be a pity, you know, to take him away from his work," she added next instant; but Engelhardt was not deceived.

They drove down the length of the shed, which had small pens attached on either side, with a kind of port-hole opening into each. Out of these port-holes there kept issuing shorn sheep, which ran down little sloping boards, and thus filled the pens. At one of the latter Naomi pulled up. It contained twice as many sheep as any other pen, and a good half of them were cut and bleeding. The pens were all numbered, and this one was number nineteen.

"Bear that in mind," said Naomi. "Nineteen!"

Engelhardt looked at her. Her face was flushed and her voice unusually quiet and hard. But she drove on without another word, save of general explanation.

"Each man has his pen," she said, "and shears his sheep just inside those holes. Then the boss of the shed comes round with his note-book, counts out the pens, and enters the number of sheep to the number of each pen. If a shearer cuts his sheep about much, or leaves a lot of wool on, he just runs that man's pen—doesn't count 'em at all. At least, he ought to. It seems he doesn't always do it."

Again her tone was a singular mixture of hard and soft.

"Mr. Gilroy is over the shed, isn't he?" said Engelhardt, a little injudiciously.

"He is," returned Naomi, and that was all.

They alighted from the buggy at the farther end of the shed, where huge doors stood open, showing a confused stack of wool-bales within, and Sanderson, the store-keeper, engaged in branding them with stencil and tar-brush. He took off his wide-awake to Naomi, and winked at the piano-tuner. The near-sighted youth was also there, and he came out to take charge of the pair, while Engelhardt entered the shed at Naomi's skirts.

Beyond the bales was the machine which turned them out. Here the two wool-pressers were hard at work and streaming with perspiration. Naomi paused to see a bale pressed down and sewn up. Then she led her companion on to where the wool-pickers were busy at side tables, and the wool-sorter at another table which stood across the shed in a commanding position, with a long line of shearers at work to right and left, and an equally long pen full of unshorn sheep between them. The wool-sorter's seemed the softest job in the shed. Boys brought him fleeces—perhaps a dozen a minute—flung them out upon the table, and rolled them up again into neat bundles swiftly tied with string. These bundles the wool-sorter merely tossed over his shoulder into one or other of the five or six bins at his back.

"He gets a pound a thousand fleeces," Naomi whispered, "and we shear something over eighty thousand sheep. He will take away a check of eighty odd pounds for his six weeks' work."

"And what about the shearers?"

"A pound a hundred. Some of them will go away with forty or fifty pounds."

"It beats piano-tuning," said Engelhardt, with a laugh. They crossed an open space, mounted a few steps, and began threading their way down the left-hand aisle, between the shearers and the pen from which they had to help themselves to woolly sheep. The air was heavy with the smell of fleeces, and not unmusical with the constant swish and chink of forty pairs of shears.

"Well, Harry?" said Naomi, to the second man they came to. "Harry is an old friend of mine, Mr. Engelhardt—he was here in the old days. Mr. Engelhardt is a new friend, Harry, but a very good one, for all that. How are you getting on? What's your top-score?"

"Ninety-one, miss—I shore ninety-one yesterday."

"And a very good top-score, too, Harry. I'd rather spend three months over the shearing than have sheep cut about and wool left on. What was that number I asked you to keep in mind, Mr. Engelhardt?"

"Nineteen, Miss Pryse."

"Ah, yes! Who's number nineteen, Harry?"

Harry grinned.

"They call him the ringer of the shed, miss."

"Oh, indeed. That means the fastest shearer, Mr. Engelhardt—the man who runs rings round the rest, eh, Harry? What's his top-score, do you suppose?"

"Something over two hundred."

"I thought as much. And his name?"

"Simons, miss."

"Point him out, Harry."

"Why, there he is; that big chap now helping himself to a woolly."

They turned and saw a huge fellow drag out an unshorn sheep by the leg, and fling it against his moleskins with a clearly unnecessary violence and cruelty.

"Come on, Mr. Engelhardt," said Naomi, in her driest tones; "I have a word to say to the ringer of the shed. I rather think he won't ring much longer."

They walked on and watched the long man at his work. It was the work of a ruffian. The shearer next him had started on a new sheep simultaneously, and was on farther than the brisket when the ringer had reached the buttocks. On the brisket of the ringer's sheep a slit of livid blue had already filled with blood, and blood started from other places as he went slashing on. He was either too intent or too insolent to take the least heed of the lady and the young man watching him. The young man's heart was going like a clock in the night, and he was sufficiently ashamed of it. As for Naomi, she was visibly boiling over, but she held her tongue until the sheep rose bleeding from its fleece. Then, as the man was about to let the poor thing go, she darted between it and the hole.

"Tar here on the brisket!" she called down the board.

A boy came at a run and dabbed the wounds.

"Why didn't you call him yourself?" she then asked sternly of the man, still detaining his sheep.

"What business is that of yours?" he returned, impudently.

"That you will see presently. How many sheep did you shear yesterday?"

"Two hundred and two."

"And the day before?"

"Two hundred and five."

"That will do. It's too much, my man, you can't do it properly. I've had a look at your sheep, and I mean to run your pen. What's more, if you don't intend to go slower and do better, you may throw down your shears this minute!"

The man had slowly lifted himself to something like his full height, which was enormous. So were his rounded shoulders and his long hairy arms and hands. So was his face, with its huge hook-nose and its mouthful of yellow teeth. These were showing in an insolent yet savage grin, when a good thing happened at a very good time.

A bell sounded, and someone sang out, "Smoke-oh!"

Instantly many pairs of shears were dropped; in the ensuing two minutes the rest followed, as each man finished the sheep he was engaged on when the bell rang. Thus the swish and tinkle of the shears changed swiftly to a hum of conversation mingled with deep-drawn sighs. And this stopped suddenly, miraculously, as the shed opened its eyes and ears to the scene going forward between its notorious ringer and Naomi Pryse, the owner of the run.

In another moment men with pipes in their hands and sweat on their brows were edging toward the pair from right and left.

"Your name, I think, is Simons?" Naomi was saying, coolly, but so that all who had a mind might hear her. "I have no more to say to you, Simons, except that you will shear properly or go where they like their sheep to have lumps of flesh taken out and lumps of wool left on."

"Since when have you been over the board, miss?" asked Simons, a little more civilly under the eyes of his mates.

"I am not over the board," said Naomi, hotly, "but I am over the man who is."

She received instant cause to regret this speech.

"We wish you was!" cried two or three. "You wouldn't make a blooming mull of things, you wouldn't!"

"I'll take my orders from Mr. Gilroy, and from nobody else," said Simons, defiantly.

"Well, you may take fair warning from me."

"That's as I like."

"It's as I like," said Naomi. "And look here, I won't waste more words upon you and I won't stand your impertinence. Better throw down your shears now—for I've done with you—before I call upon your mates to take them from you."

"We don't need calling, miss, not we!"

Half a dozen fine fellows had stepped forward, with Harry at their head, and the affair was over. Simons had flung his shears on the floor with a clatter and a curse, and was striding out of the shed amid the hisses and imprecations of his comrades.

Naomi would have got away, too, for she had had more than enough of the whole business, but this was not so easy. Someone raised three cheers for her. They were given with a roar that shook the iron roof like thunder. And to cap all this a gray old shearer planted himself in her path.

"It's just this way, miss," said he. "We liked Simons little enough, but, begging your pardon, we like Mr. Gilroy less. He doesn't know how to treat us at all. He has no idea of bossing a shed like this. And mark my words, miss, unless you remove that man, and give us some smarter gentleman like, say, young Mr. Chester—"

"Ay, Chester'll do!"

"He knows his business!"

"He's a man, he is—"

"And the man for us!"

"Unless you give us someone more to our fancy, like young Mr. Chester," concluded the old man, doing his best to pacify his mates with look and gesture, "there'll be further trouble. This is only the beginning. There'll be trouble, and maybe worse, until you make a change."

Naomi felt inexpressibly uncomfortable.

"Mr. Gilroy is the manager of this station," said she, for once with a slight tremor in her voice. "Any difference that you have with him, you must fight it out between you. I am quite sure that he means to be just. I, at any rate, must interfere no more. I am sorry I interfered at all."

So they let her go at last, the piano-tuner following close upon her heels. He had stuck to her all the time with shut mouth and twitching fingers, ready for anything, as he was ready still. And the first person these two encountered in the open air was Gilroy himself, with so white a face and such busy lips that they hardly required him to tell them he had heard all.

"I am very sorry, Monty," said the girl, in a distressed tone which highly surprised her companion; "but I simply couldn't help it. You can't stand by and see a sheep cut to pieces without opening your mouth. Yet I know I was at fault."

"It's not much good knowing it now," returned Gilroy, ungraciously, as he rolled along at her side; "you should have thought of that first. As it is, you've given me away to the shed, and made a tough job twice as tough as it was before."

"I really am very sorry, Monty. I know I oughtn't to have interfered at all. At the same time, the man deserved sending away, and I am sure you would have been the first to send him had you seen what I saw. I know I should have waited and spoken to you; but I shall keep away from the shed in future."

"That won't undo this morning's mischief. I heard what the brutes said to you!"

"Then you must have heard what I said to them. Don't try to make me out worse than I am, Monty."

She laid her hand upon his arm, and Engelhardt, to his horror, saw tears on her lashes. Gilroy, however, would not look at her. Instead, he hailed the store-keeper, who had passed them on his way to the huts.

"Make out Simons's account, Sandy," he shouted at the top of his voice, "and give him his check. Miss Pryse has thought fit to sack him over my head!"

Instantly her penitence froze to scorn.

"That was unnecessary," she said, in the same quiet tone she had employed toward the shearer, but dropping her arm and halting dead as she spoke. "If this is the way you treat the men, no wonder you can't manage them. Come, Mr. Engelhardt!"

And with this they turned their back on the manager, but not on the shed; that was not Naomi's way at all. She was pre-eminently one to be led, not driven, and she remained upon the scene, showing Engelhardt everything, and explaining the minutest details for his benefit, much longer than she would have dreamt of staying in the ordinary course of affairs. This involved luncheon in the manager's hut, at which meal Naomi appeared in the highest spirits, cracking jokes with Sanderson, chaffing the boy in spectacles, and clinking pannikins with everyone but the manager himself. The latter left early, after steadily sulking behind his plate, with his beard in his waistcoat and his yellow head presented like a bull's. Tom Chester was not there at all. Engelhardt was sorry, though the others treated him well enough to-day—Sanderson even cutting up his meat for him. It was three o'clock before Naomi and he started homeward in the old Shanghai.

With the wool-shed left a mile behind, they overtook a huge horseman leading a spare horse.

"That's our friend Simons," said Naomi. "I wonder what sort of a greeting he'll give me. None at all, I should imagine."

She was wrong. The shearer reined up on one side of the track, and gave her a low bow, wide-awake in hand, and with it a kind of a glaring grin that made his teeth stand out like brass-headed nails in the afternoon sunshine. Naomi laughed as they drove on.

"Pretty, wasn't it? That man loves me to distraction, I should say. On the whole we may claim to have had a rather lively day. First came that young lady on the near side, who's behaving herself so angelically now; and then the swingle-tree, which they've fixed up well enough to see us through this afternoon at any rate. Next there was our friend Simons; and after him, poor dear Monty Gilroy—who had cause to complain, mind you, Mr. Engelhardt. We mustn't forget that I had no sort of right to interfere. And now, unless I'm very much mistaken, we're on the point of meeting two more of our particular friends."

In fact, a couple of tramps were approaching, swag on back, with the slow swinging stride of their kind. Engelhardt colored hotly as he recognized the ruffians of the day before. They were walking on opposite sides of the track, and as the buggy cut between them the fat man unpocketed one hand and saluted them as they passed.

"Not got a larger size yet?" he shouted out. "Why, that ain't a man at all!"

The poor piano-tuner felt red to his toes, and held his tongue with exceeding difficulty. But, as usual, Naomi and her laugh came to his rescue.

"How polite our friends are, to be sure! A bow here and a salute there! Birds of a feather, too, if ever I saw any; you might look round, Mr. Engelhardt, and see if they're flocking together."

"They are," said he, next minute.

Then Naomi looked for herself. They were descending a slight incline, and, sure enough, on top of the ridge stood the two tramps and the mounted shearer. Stamped clean against the sky, it looked much as though horses and men had been carved out of a single slab of ebony.

CHAPTER VIII

"THREE SHADOWS"

That night the piano-tuner came out in quite a new character, and with immediate success. He began repeating poetry in the moonlit veranda, and Naomi let him go on for an hour and a half; indeed, she made him; for she was in secret tribulation over one or two things that had happened during the day, and only too thankful, therefore, to be taken out of herself and made to think on other matters. Engelhardt did all this for her, and in so doing furthered his own advantage, too, almost as much as his own pleasure. At all events, Naomi took to her room a livelier interest in the piano-tuner than she had felt hitherto, while her own troubles were left, with her boots, outside the door.

It was true she had been interested in him from the beginning. He had so very soon revealed to her what she had never come in contact with before—a highly sensitized specimen of the artistic temperament. She did not know it by this name, or by any name at all; but she was not the less alive to his little group of interesting peculiarities, because of her inability to label the lot with one phrase. They interested her the more for that very reason; just as her instinct as to the possibilities that were in him was all the stronger for her incapacity to reason out her conviction in a satisfactory manner. Her intellectual experience was limited to a degree; but she had seen success in his face; and she now heard it in his voice when he quoted verses to her, so beautifully that she was delighted to listen whether she followed him or not. Her faith in him was sweetly unreasonable, but it was immensely strong. She was ready and even eager to back him heavily; and there are those who would rather have one brave girl do that on instinct, than win the votes of a hundred clear heads, basing their support upon a logical calculation.

For reasons of her own, however, Naomi decided overnight to take her visitor a little less seriously to his face. She had been too confidential with him concerning station affairs past and present; that she must drop, and at the same time discourage him from opening his heart to her, as he was beginning to do, on the slightest provocation. These resolutions would impose a taboo on nearly all the subjects they had found in common. She quite saw that, and she thought it just as well. Too much sympathy with this young man might be bad for him. Naomi realized this somewhat suddenly in the night, and it kept her awake rather longer than she liked. But she rose next morning fully resolved to eschew conversation of too sympathetic a character, and to encourage her young friend in quotations from the poets instead. Obviously this was quite as great a pleasure to him, while it was a much safer one—or so Naomi thought in her innocence. But then it was a very genuine pleasure to her, too, because the poetry was entirely new to her, and her many-sided young man knew so much and repeated it so charmingly.

It was incredible, indeed, what a number of the poets of all ages he had at his finger-ends, and how justly he rendered their choicest numbers. Their very names were mostly new to Naomi. There was consequently an aboriginal barbarity about many of her comments and criticisms, and more than once the piano-tuner found it impossible to sit still and hear her out. This was notably the case at their second poetical séance, when Naomi had got over her private depression on the one hand, and was full of her new intentions toward the piano-tuner on the other. He would jump out of his chair, and fume up and down the veranda, running his five available fingers through his hair until the black shock stood on end. It was at these moments that Naomi liked him best.

He had been giving her "Tears, idle tears" (because she had "heard of Tennyson," she said) on the Wednesday morning in the veranda facing the station-yard. He had recited the great verses with a force and feeling all his own. Over one of them in particular his voice had quivered with emotion. It was the dear emotion of an æsthetic soul touched to the quick by the sheer beauty of the idea and its words. And Naomi said:

"That's jolly; but you don't call it poetry, do you?"

His eyes dried in an instant. Then they opened as wide as they would go. He was speechless.

"It doesn't rhyme, you know," Naomi explained, cheerfully.

"No," said Engelhardt, gazing at her severely. "It isn't meant to; it's blank verse."

"It's blank bad verse, if you ask me," said Naomi Pryse, with a nod that was meant to finish him; but it only lifted him out of his chair.

"Well, upon my word," said the piano-tuner, striding noisily up and down, as Naomi laughed. "Upon my word!"

"Please make me understand," pleaded the girl, with a humility that meant mischief, if he had only been listening; but he was still wrestling with his exasperation. "I can't help being ignorant, you know," she added, as though hurt.

"You can help it—that's just it!" he answered, bitterly. "I've been telling you one of the most beautiful things that Tennyson himself ever wrote, and you say it isn't verse. Verse, forsooth! It's poetry—it's gorgeous poetry!"

"It may be gorgeous, but I don't call it poetry unless it rhymes," said Naomi, stoutly. "Gordon always does."

Gordon, the Australian poet, she was forever throwing at his head, as the equal of any of his English bards. They had already had a heated argument about Gordon. Therefore Engelhardt said merely:

"You're joking, of course?"

"I am doing nothing of the sort."

"Then pray what do you call Shakespeare"—pausing in front of her with his hand in his pocket—"poetry or prose?"

"Prose, of course."

"Because it doesn't rhyme?"

"Exactly."

"And why do you suppose it's chopped up into lines?"

"Oh, I don't know—to moisten it perhaps."

"I beg your pardon?"

"To make it less dry."

"Ah! Then it doesn't occur to you that there might be some law which decreed the end of a line after a certain number of beats, or notes—exactly like the end of a bar of music, in fact?"

"Certainly not," said Naomi. There was a touch of indignation in this denial. He shrugged his shoulders and then turned them upon the girl, and stood glowering out upon the yard. Behind his back Naomi went into fits of silent laughter, which luckily she had overcome before he wheeled round suddenly with a face full of eager determination. His heart now appeared set upon convincing her that verse might be blank. And for half an hour he stood beating his left hand in the air, and declaiming, in feet, certain orations of Hamlet, until Mrs. Potter, the cook-laundress, came out of the kitchen to protect her young mistress if necessary. It was not necessary. The broken-armed gentleman was standing over her, shaking his fist and talking at the top of his voice; but Miss Pryse was all smiles and apparent contentment; and, indeed, she behaved much better for awhile, and did her best to understand. But presently she began to complain of the "quotations" (for he was operating on the famous soliloquy), and to profane the whole subject. And the question of blank verse was discussed between them no more.

She could be so good, too, when she liked, so appreciative, so sympathetic, so understanding. But she never liked very long. He had a tendency to run to love-poems, and after listening to five or six with every sign of approval and delight, Naomi would suddenly become flippant at the sixth or seventh. On one occasion, when she had turned him on by her own act aforethought, and been given a taste of several past-masters of the lyric, from Waller to Locker, and including a poem of Browning's which she allowed herself to be made to understand, she inquired of Engelhardt whether he had ever read anything by "a man called Swinton."

"Swinburne," suggested Engelhardt.

"Are you sure?" said Naomi, jealously. "I believe it's Swinton. I'm prepared to bet you that it is!"

"Where have you come across his name?" the piano-tuner said, smiling as he shook his head.

"In the preface to Gordon's poems."

Engelhardt groaned.

"It mentions Swinton—what are you laughing at? All right! I'll get the book and settle it!"

She came back laughing herself.

"Well?" said Engelhardt.

"You know too much! Not that I should accept anything that preface says as conclusive. It has the cheek to say that Gordon was under his influence. You give me something of his, and we'll soon see."

"Something of Swinburne's?"

"Oh, you needn't put on side because you happen to be right according to a preface. I'll write and ask The Australasian! Yes, of course I mean something of his."

Engelhardt reflected. "There's a poem called 'A Leave-taking,'" said he, tentatively, at length.

"Then trot it out," said Naomi; and she set herself to listen with so unsympathetic an expression on her pretty face, that he was obliged to look the other way before he could begin. The contrary was usually the case. However, he managed to get under way:

"Let us go hence, my songs; she will not hear.

Let us go hence together without fear;
Keep silence now, for singing-time is over,
And over all old things and all things dear.
She loves not you nor me as all we love her.
Yea, though we sang as angels in her ear,
She would not hear.

"Let us rise up and part; she will not know.
Let us go seaward as the great winds go,
Full of blown sand and foam; what help is there?
There is no help, for all these things are so,
And all the world is bitter as a tear.
And how these things are, though ye strove to show
She would not know.

"Let us go home and hence; she will not weep—"

"Stop a moment," said Naomi, "I'm in a difficulty. I can't go on listening until I know something."

"Until you know what?" said Engelhardt, who did not like being interrupted.

"Who it's all about—who she is!" cried Naomi, inquisitively.

"Who—she—is," repeated the piano-tuner, talking aloud to himself.

"Yes, exactly; who is she?"

"As if it mattered!" Engelhardt went on in the same aside. "However, who do you say she is?"

"I? She may be his grandmother for all I know. I'm asking you."

"I know you are. I was prepared for you to ask me anything else."

"Were you? Then why is she such an obstinate old party, anyway? She won't hear and she won't know. What will she do? Now it seems that you can't even make her cry! 'She will not weep' was where you'd got to. As you seem unable to answer my questions, you'd better go on till she does."

"I'm so likely to go on," said Engelhardt, getting up.

Naomi relented a little.

"Forgive me, Mr. Engelhardt; I've been behaving horribly. I'm sorry I spoke at all, only I did so want to know who she was."

"I don't know myself."

"I was sure you didn't!"

"What's more, I don't care. What has it got to do with the merits of the poem?"

"I won't presume to say. I only know that it makes all the difference to my interest in the poem."

"But why?"

"Because I want to know what she was like."

"But surely to goodness," cried Engelhardt, "you can imagine her, can't you? You're meant to fill her in to your own fancy. You pays your money and you takes your choice."

"I get precious little for my money," remarked Naomi, pertinently, "if I have to do the filling in for myself!"

Engelhardt had been striding to and fro. Now he stopped pityingly in front of the chair in which this sweet Philistine was sitting unashamed.

"Do you mean to say that you like to have every little thing told you in black and white?"

"Of course I do. The more the better."

"And absolutely nothing left to your own imagination?"

"Certainly not. The idea!"

He turned away from her with a shrug of his shoulders, and quickened his stride up and down the veranda. He was visibly annoyed. She watched him with eyes full of glee.

"I do love to make you lose your wool!" she informed him in a minute or two, with a sudden attack of candor. "I like you best when you give me up and wash your hands of me!"

This cleared his brow instantaneously, and brought him back to her chair with a smile.

"Why so, Miss Pryse?"

"Must I tell you?"

"Please."

"Then it's because you forget yourself, and me, too, when I rile you; and you're delightful whenever you do that, Mr. Engelhardt."

Naomi regretted her words next moment; but it was too late to unsay them. He went on smiling, it is true, but his smile was no longer naïve and unconsidered; no more were his recitations during the next few hours. His audience did her worst to provoke him out of himself, but she could not manage it. Then she tried the other extreme, and became more enthusiastic than himself over this and that, but he would not be with her; he had retired into the lair of his own self-consciousness, and there was no tempting him out any more. When he did come out of himself, it was neither by his own will nor her management, and the moment was a startling one for them both.

It was late in the afternoon of that same Wednesday. They were sitting, as usual, in the veranda which overlooked not the station-yard but the boundless plains, and they were sitting in silence and wide apart. They had not quarrelled; but Engelhardt had made up his mind to decamp. He had reasoned the whole thing out in a spirit of mere common-sense; yet he was reasoning with himself still, as he sat in the quiet veranda; he thought it probable that he should go on with his reasoning—with the same piece of reasoning—until his dying hour. He looked worried. He was certainly worrying Naomi, and annoying her considerably. She had given up trying to take him out of himself, but she knew that he liked to hear himself saying poetry, and she felt perfectly ready to listen if it would do him any good. Of course she was not herself anxious to hear him. It was entirely for his sake that she put down the book she was reading, and broached the subject at last.

"Have you quite exhausted the poetry that you know by heart, Mr. Engelhardt?"

"Quite, I'm afraid, Miss Pryse; and I'm sure you must be thankful to hear it."

"Now you're fishing," said Naomi, with a smile (not one of her sweetest); "we've quarrelled about all your precious poets, it's true, but that's why I want you to trot out another. I'm dying for another quarrel, don't you see? Out with somebody fresh, and let me have shies at him!"

"But I don't know them all off by heart—I'm not a walking Golden Treasury, you know."

"Think!" commanded Naomi. When she did this there was no disobeying her. He had found out that already.

"Have you ever heard of Rossetti—Dante Gabriel?"

"Kill whose cat?" cried Naomi.

He repeated the poet's name in full. She shook her head. She was smiling now, and kindly, for she had got her way.

"There is one little thing of his—but a beauty—that I once learnt," Engelhardt said, doubtfully. "Mind, I'm not sure that I can remember it, and I won't spoil it if I can't; no more must you spoil it, if I can."

"Is there some sacred association, then?"

He laughed. "No, indeed! There's more of a sacrilegious association, for I once swore that the first song I composed should be a setting for these words."

"Remember, you've got to dedicate it to me! What's the name of the thing?"

"'Three Shadows.'"

"Let's have them, then."

"Very well. But I love it! You must promise not to laugh."

"Begin," she said, sternly, and he began:

"I looked and saw your eyes
In the shadow of your hair,
As the traveller sees the stream
In the shadow of the wood;
And I said, 'My faint heart sighs
Ah me! to linger there,
To drink deep and to dream
In that sweet solitude.'"

"Go on," said Naomi, with approval. "I hope you don't see all that; but please go on."

He had got thus far with his face raised steadfastly to hers, for he had left his chair and seated himself on the edge of the veranda, at her feet, before beginning. He went on without wincing or lowering his eyes:

"I looked and saw your heart
In the shadow of your eyes,
As a seeker sees the gold
In the shadow of the stream;
And I said, 'Ah me! what art
Should win the immortal prize,
Whose want must make life cold
And heaven a hollow dream?'"

"Surely not as bad as all that?" said Naomi, laughing. He had never recited anything so feelingly, so slowly, with such a look in his eyes. There was occasion to laugh, obviously.

"Am I to go on," said Engelhardt, in desperate earnest, "or am I not?"

"Go on, of course! I am most anxious to know what else you saw."

But the temptation to lower the eyes was now hers; his look was so hard to face, his voice was grown so soft.

"I looked and saw your love
In the shadow of your heart,
As a diver sees the pearl
In the shadow of the sea;
And I murmured, not above
My breath, but all apart—"

Here he stopped. Her eyes were shining. He could not see this, because his own were dim.

"Go on," she said, nodding violently, "do go on!"

"That's all I remember."

"Nonsense! What did you murmur?"

"I forget."

"You do no such thing."

"I've said all I mean to say."

"But not all I mean you to. I will have the lot."

And, after all, his were the eyes to fall; but in a moment they had leapt up again to her face with a sudden reckless flash.

"There are only two more lines," he said; "you had much better not know them."

"I must," said she. "What are they?"

"Ah! you can love, true girl,
And is your love for me?"

"No, I'm afraid not," said Naomi, at last.

"I thought not."

"Nor for anybody else—nor for anybody else!"

She was leaning over him, and one of her hands had fallen upon his neck—so kindly—so naturally—like a mother's upon her child.

"Then you are not in love with anybody else!" he cried, joyously. "You are not engaged!"

"Yes," she answered, sadly. "I am engaged."

Then Naomi learnt how it feels to quench the fire in joyous eyes, and to wrinkle a hopeful young face with the lines of anguish and despair. She could not bear it. She took the head of untidy hair between her two soft hands, and pressed it down upon the open book on her knees until the haunting eyes looked into hers no more. And as a mother soothes her child, so she stroked him, and patted him, and murmured over him, until he could speak to her calmly.

"Who is he?" whispered Engelhardt, drawing away from her at last, and gazing up into her face with a firm lip. "What is he? Where is he? I want to know everything!"

"Then look over your shoulder, and you will see him for yourself."

A horseman had indeed ridden round the corner of the house, noiselessly in the heavy sand. Monty Gilroy sat frowning at them both from his saddle.

CHAPTER IX

NO HOPE FOR HIM

"I'm afraid I have interrupted a very interesting conversation?" said Gilroy, showing his teeth through his beard.

Naomi smiled coolly.

"What if I say that you have, Monty?"

"Then I'm sorry, but it can't be helped," replied the manager, jumping off his horse, and hanging the bridle over a hook on one of the veranda-posts.

"Ah, I thought as much," said Naomi, dryly. She held out her hand, however, as she spoke.

But Gilroy had stopped before setting foot in the veranda. He stood glaring at Engelhardt, who was not looking at him, but at the fading sky-line away beyond the sand and scrub, and with a dazed expression upon his pale, eager face. The piano-tuner had not risen; he had merely turned round where he sat, at the sound of Gilroy's voice.

Now, however, he seemed neither to see nor to heed the manager, though the latter was towering over him, white with mortification.

"Now then, Mr. Piano-tuner, jump up and clear; I've ridden over to see Miss Pryse on urgent business—"

"Leaving your manners behind you, evidently," observed that young lady, "or I think you would hardly be ordering my visitors out of my veranda and my presence!"

"Then will you speak to the fellow?" said Gilroy, sulkily. "He seems deaf, and I haven't ridden in for my own amusement. I tell you it's an important matter, Naomi."

"Mr. Engelhardt!" said Naomi, gently. He turned at once. "Mr. Gilroy," she went on to explain, "has come from the shed to see me about something or other. Will you leave us for a little while?"

"Certainly, Miss Pryse." He rose in sudden confusion. "I—I beg your pardon. I was thinking of something else."

It was only Naomi's pardon that he begged. He had not looked twice at Gilroy; but as he rounded the corner of the building, he glanced sharply over his shoulder. He could not help it. He felt instinctively that a glimpse of their lovers' greeting would do something toward his cure. All that he saw, however, was Naomi with her back to the wall, and her hands laid firmly upon the wicker chair-back where her head had rested a moment before. Across this barrier Gilroy had opened so vehement a fire upon her that Engelhardt thought twice about leaving them alone together. As he hesitated, however, the girl shot him a glance which commanded him to be gone, while it as plainly intimated her perfect ability to take care of herself.

Once out of her sight, the piano-tuner turned a resolute back upon the homestead, determining to get right away from it for the time being—to get away and to think. He did not, however, plunge into the plantation of pines, in which Naomi and he had often wandered during these last few days, that seemed a happy lifetime to him now that he felt they were over. He took the broad, sandy way which led past the stables to the men's hut on the left, and to the stock-yards on the right. Behind the yards the sun was setting, the platform for the pithing of bullocks, and the windlass for raising their carcasses, standing out sharp and black against the flaming sky; and still farther to the right, where there were sheep-yards also, a small yellow cloud rose against the pink like a pillar of sand. Engelhardt knew little enough of station life, but he saw that somebody was yarding-up a mob of sheep for the night. He went on to have a look at the job, which was over, however, before he reached the spot. Three horses were trotting off in the direction of the horse-paddock, while, coming away from the yard, carrying their saddles and bridles, were two of the station hands and the overseer, Tom Chester.

"Hulloa, Engelhardt, still here?" said the latter, cheerily, as they met. "How goes the arm?"

"First-rate, thanks. I'm off to-morrow."

"Yes? Come on back to the homestead, and help me shave and brush up. I've been mustering seventeen miles from the shed. We've run the mob into these yards for the night, and I'm roosting in the barracks."

"So is Mr. Gilroy, I fancy."

"The devil he is! Has he come in from the shed, then?"

"Yes; within the last ten minutes."

Chester looked black.

"You didn't hear what for, I suppose?"

"To speak to Miss Pryse about some important matter; that's all I know."

"I should have thought they'd had enough to say to each other yesterday, to last Gilroy for a bit. I'm mustering, you know; but I heard all about it when I got back to the shed last night. Some of the men came to me in a sort of deputation. They hate Gilroy about as much as I do, and they want him out of that. If he's a sensible man he's come in to chuck up the sponge himself."

Tom Chester flung his saddle and bridle over the rail as they passed the stable, and walked on to the station-yard, and across it to the little white barracks, without another word. Engelhardt followed him into his room and sat down on the bed. He felt that they understood one another. That was what made him say, while Chester was stropping his razor:

"You don't love Gilroy, I imagine."

"No, I don't," replied Tom Chester, after a pause.

"But Miss Pryse does!" Engelhardt exclaimed, bitterly.

The other made a longer pause. He was lathering his chin. "Not she," said Tom, coolly, at length.

"Not! But she's engaged to him, I hear!"

"There's a sort of understanding."

"Only an understanding?"

"Well, she doesn't wear a ring, for one thing."

"I wish you would tell me just how it stands," said Engelhardt, inquisitively. His heart was beating, nevertheless.

"Tell you?" said Tom Chester, looking only into the glass as he flourished his razor. "Why, certainly. I don't wonder at your wanting to know how a fine girl like that could go and engage herself to a God-forsaken image like Gilroy. I don't know, mind you. I wasn't here in Mr. Pryse's time; but everyone says he was a good sort, and that the worse thing he ever did was to take on Gilroy, just because he was some sort of relation of his dead wife's. He's second cousin to Miss Pryse, that's what Gilroy is; but he was overseer here when the boss was his own manager, and when he died Gilroy got the management, naturally. Well, and then he got the girl, too—the Lord knows how. She knew that her father thought well of the skunk, and no doubt she herself felt it was the easiest way out of her responsibilities and difficulties. Ay, she was a year or two younger then than she is now, and he got the promise of her; but I'll bet you an even dollar he never gets her to keep."

The piano-tuner had with difficulty sat still upon the bed, as he listened to this seemingly impartial version of the engagement which had numbed his spirit from the moment he heard of it. Tom Chester had spoken with many pauses, filled by the tinkle of his razor against a healthy beard three days old. When he offered to bet the dollar, he was already putting the razor away in its case.

"I won't take you," said Engelhardt. "You don't think she'll marry him, then?" he added, anxiously.

"Tar here on the brisket," remarked Chester, in the shearer's formula, as he dabbed at a cut that he had discovered under his right jaw. "What's that! Marry him? No; of course she won't."

Engelhardt waited while the overseer performed elaborate ablutions and changed his clothes. Then they crossed over together to the front veranda, which was empty; but as they went round to the back the sound of voices came fast enough to their ears. The owner and her manager were still talking in the back veranda, which was now in darkness, and their voices were still raised. It was Tom Chester's smile, however, that helped Engelhardt to grasp the full significance of the words that met their ears. Gilroy was speaking.

"All right, Naomi! You know best, no doubt. You mean to paddle your own canoe, you say, and that's all very well; but if Tom Chester remains on at the shed there'll be a row, I tell you straight."

"Between whom?" Naomi inquired.

"Between Tom Chester and me. I tell you he's stirring up the men against me! You yourself did mischief enough yesterday; but when he came in he made bad worse. It may be an undignified thing to do, for the boss of the shed; but I can't help that, I shall have to fight him."

"Fight whom?" said Chester, in a tone of interest, as he and Engelhardt came upon the scene together.

"You," replied Naomi, promptly. "You have arrived in the nick of time, Mr. Chester. I am sorry to hear that you two don't hit it off together at the shed."

"So that's it, is it?" said Tom Chester, quietly, glancing from the girl to Gilroy, who had not opened his mouth. "And you're prepared to hit it off somewhere else, are you? I'm quite ready. I have been wanting to hit it off with you, Gilroy, ever since I've known you."

His meaning was as plain as an italicised joke. They all waited for the manager's reply.

"Indeed!" said he, at length, out of the kindly dark that hid the color of his face. "So you expect me to answer you before Miss Pryse, do you?"

"On the contrary, I'd far rather you came down to the stables and answered me there. But you might repeat before Miss Pryse whatever it is you were telling her about me behind my back."

"I shall do nothing of the sort."

"Then I must do it for you," said Naomi, firmly.

"Do," said Gilroy. And diving his hands deep into his cross-pockets, he swaggered off the scene with his horse at his heels and his arm through the reins.

"I think I can guess the kind of thing, Miss Pryse," Tom Chester waited to say; "you needn't trouble to tell me, thank you." A moment later he had followed the manager, and the piano-tuner was following Tom; but Naomi Pryse remained where she was. She had not lifted a finger to prevent the fight which, as she saw for herself, was a good deal more imminent than he had imagined who warned her of it five minutes before.

"Will you take off your coat?" said Chester, as he caught up to Gilroy between homestead and stables.

"Is it likely?" queried Gilroy, without looking round.

"That depends whether you're a man. The light's the same for both. There are lanterns in the stables, whether or no. Will you take off your coat when we get there?"

"To you? Manager and overseer? Don't be a fool, Tom."

"I'll show you who's the fool in a brace of shakes," said Tom Chester, following Gilroy with a swelling chest. "I never thought you had much pluck, but, by God, I don't believe you've got the pluck of a louse!"

Gilroy led on his horse without answering.

"Have you got the pluck of a louse?" the overseer sang into his ear. Gilroy was trembling, but he turned as they reached the stable.

"Take off your coat, then," said he, doggedly; "I'll leave mine inside."

Gilroy led his horse into the stable. Instead of taking off his coat, however, Tom Chester stood waiting with his arms akimbo and his eyes upon the open stable-door.

"Aren't you going to take it off?" said an eager yet nervous voice at his side. "Don't you mean to fight him after all?"

It was the piano-tuner, whose desire to see the manager soundly thrashed was at war with his innate dread of anything approaching a violent scene. He could be violent himself when his blood was up, but in his normal state the mere sound of high words made him miserable.

"Hulloa! I didn't see that you were there," remarked Chester, with a glance at the queer little figure beside him. "Lord, yes; I'll fight him if he's game, but I won't believe that till I see it, so we'll let him strip first. The fellow hasn't got the pluck of— I knew he hadn't! That's just what I should have expected of him!"

Before Engelhardt could realize what was happening, a horse had emerged from the shadow of the stable-door, a man's head and wide-awake had risen behind its ears as they cleared the lintel, and Gilroy, with a smack of his whip on the horse's flank and a cut and a curse at Tom Chester, was disappearing in the dusk at a gallop. Chester had sprung forward, but he was not quick enough. When the cut had fallen short of him, he gathered himself together for one moment, as though to give chase on foot; then stood at ease and watched the rider out of sight.

"Next time, my friend," said he, "you won't get the option of standing up to me. No; by the Lord, I'll take him by the scruff of his dirty neck, and I'll take the very whip he's got in his hand now, and I'll hide him within an inch of his miserable life. That's the way we treat curs in these parts, d'ye see? Come on, Engelhardt. No, we'll stop and see which road he takes when he gets to the gate. I can just see him opening it now. I might have caught him up there if I'd thought. Ah! he's shaking his fist at us; he shall smell mine before he's a day older! And he's taken the township track; he'll come back to the shed as drunk as a fool, and if the men don't dip him in the dam I shall be very much surprised."

"And Miss Pryse is going to marry a creature like that," cried Engelhardt, as they walked back to the house.

"Not she," said Chester, confidently.

"Yet there's a sort of engagement."

"There is; but it would be broken off to-morrow if I were to tell Miss Pryse to-night of the mess he's making of everything out at the shed. The men do what they like with him, and he goes dropping upon the harmless inoffensive ones, and fining them and running their sheep; whereas he daren't have said a word to that fellow Simons, not to save his life. I tell you there'd have been a strike last night if it hadn't been for me. The men appealed to me, and I said what I thought. So his nibs sends me mustering again, about as far off as he can, while he comes in to get Miss Pryse to give me the sack. Of course that's what he's been after. That's the kind of man he is. But here's Miss Pryse herself in the veranda, and we'll drop the subject, d'ye see?"

Naomi herself never mentioned it. Possibly from the veranda she had seen and heard enough to enable her to guess the rest pretty accurately. However that may be, the name of Monty Gilroy never passed her lips, either now in the interval before dinner, or at that meal, during which she conversed very merrily with the two young men who faced one another on either side of her. She insisted on carving for them both, despite the protests of the more talkative of the two. She rattled on to them incessantly—if anything, to Engelhardt more than to the overseer. But there could be no question as to which of these two talked most to her. Engelhardt was even more shy and awkward than at his first meal at Taroomba, when Naomi had not been present. He disappeared immediately after dinner, and Naomi had to content herself with Tom Chester's company for the rest of the evening.

That, however, was very good company at all times, while on the present occasion Miss Pryse had matters for discussion with her overseer which rendered a private interview quite necessary. So Engelhardt was not wanted for at least an hour; but he did not come back at all. When Chester went whistling to the barracks at eleven o'clock he found the piano-tuner lying upon his bed in all his clothes.

"Hulloa, my son, are you sick?" said Tom, entering the room. The risen moon was shining in on all sides of the looking-glass.

"No, I'm well enough, thanks. I felt rather sleepy."

"You don't sound sleepy! Miss Pryse was wondering what could be the matter. She told me to tell you that you might at least have said good-night to her."

"I'll go and say it now," cried Engelhardt, bounding from the bed.

"Ah, now you're too late, you see," said Chester, laughing a little unkindly as he barred the doorway. "You didn't suppose I'd come away before I was obliged, did you? Come into my room, and I'll tell you a bit of news."

The two rooms were close together; they were divided by the narrow passage that led without step or outer door into the station-yard. It was a lined, set face that the candle lighted up when Tom Chester put a match to it; but that was only the piano-tuner's face, and Tom stood looking at his own, and the smile in the glass was peculiar and characteristic. It was not conceited; it was merely confident. The overseer of Taroomba was one of the smartest, most resolute, and confident young men in the back-blocks of New South Wales.

"The news," he said, turning away from the glass and undoing his necktie, "may surprise you, but I've expected it all along. Didn't I tell you before dinner that Miss Pryse would be breaking off her rotten engagement one of these days! Well, then, she's been and done it this very afternoon."

"Thank God!" cried Engelhardt.

"Amen," echoed Chester, with a laugh. He had paid no attention to the piano-tuner's tone and look. He was winding a keyless watch.

"And is he going on here as manager?" Engelhardt asked, presently.

"No, that's the point. Naomi seems to have told him pretty straight that she could get along without him, and on second thoughts he's taken her at her word. She got a note an hour ago to say she would never see him again. He'd sent a chap with it all the way from the township."

"Do you mean to say he isn't coming back?"

"That's the idea. You bet he had it when he shook his fist at us as he opened that gate. He was shaking his fist at the station and all hands on the place, particularly including the boss. She's to send his things and his check after him to the township, where they'll find him drunk, you mark my words. Good riddance to the cur! Of course he was going to marry her for her money; but she's tumbled to him in time, and a miss is as good as a mile any day in the week."

He finished speaking and winding his watch at the same moment. It was a gold watch, and he set it down carelessly on the dressing-table, where the candle shone upon the monogram on its back.

"He has nothing of his own?" queried Engelhardt, with jealous eyes upon the watch.

"Not a red cent," said Tom Chester, contemptuously. "He lived upon the old boss, and of course he meant to live upon his daughter after him. He was as poor as a church-mouse."

So indeed was the piano-tuner. He did not say as much, however, though the words had risen to his lips. He said no more until the overseer was actually in bed. Then a flash of inspiration caused him to ask, abruptly,

"Are you anything to do with Chester, Wilkinson, & Killick, the big wool-people down in Melbourne?"

"To do with 'em?" repeated Tom, with a smile. "Well, yes; at least, I'm Chester's son."

"I've heard that you own more Riverina stations than any other firm or company?"

"Yes; this is about the only one around here that we haven't got a finger in. That's why I came here, by the way, for a bit of experience."

"Then you don't want to marry her for her money. You'll have more than she ever will! Isn't that so?"

"What the blue blazes do you mean, Engelhardt?"

Chester had sat bolt upright in his bed. The piano-tuner was still on the foot of it, and all the fire in his being had gone into his eyes.

"Mean?" he cried. "Who cares what I mean! I tell you that she thinks more of you than ever she thought of Gilroy. She has said so to me in as many words. I tell you to go in and win!"

He was holding out his left hand.

"I intend to," said Tom Chester, taking it good-naturedly enough. "That's exactly my game, and everybody must know it, for I've been playing it fair and square in the light of day. I may lose; but I hope to win. Good-night, Engelhardt. Shall I look you up in the morning? We make a very early start, mind."

"Then you needn't trouble. But I do wish you luck!"

"Thanks, my boy. I wish myself luck, too."

Naomi's room opened upon the back veranda, and in quitting it next morning it was not unnatural that she should pause to contemplate the place where so many things had lately happened, which, she felt, must leave their mark upon her life for good or evil. It was here that she might have seen the danger of unreserved sympathy with so sensitive and enthusiastic a nature as that of the piano-tuner. Indeed, she had seen it, and made suitable resolutions on the spot; but these she had broken, and wilfully shut her eyes to that danger until the young man had told her, quite plainly enough, that he loved her. Nay, she had made him tell her that, and until he did so she had purposely withheld from him the knowledge that she was already engaged. That was the cruel part of it, the part of which she was now most sincerely ashamed. Yet some power stronger than her own will had compelled her to act as she had done, and certainly she had determined beforehand to take the first opportunity of severing all ties still existing between herself and Monty Gilroy. And it was here that she had actually broken off her engagement with him within a few minutes of her announcement of it to Hermann Engelhardt. Still she was by no means pleased with herself as she stepped out into the flood of sunshine that filled the back veranda of a morning, and saw everything as it had been overnight, even to the book she had laid aside open when Gilroy rode up. It was lying shut in the self-same spot. This little difference was the only one.

She went round to the front of the house, looking out rather nervously for Engelhardt on the way. Generally he met her in the front veranda, but this morning he was not there. Mrs. Potter was laying the breakfast-table, but she had not seen him either. She looked searchingly at her young mistress as she answered her question.

"Are you quite well, miss?" she asked at length, without preamble. "You look as though you hadn't slep' a wink all night."

"No more I have," said Naomi, calmly.

"Good gracious, miss!" cried Mrs. Potter, clapping down the plate-basket with a jingle. "Whatever has been the matter? That nasty toothache, I'll be bound!"

"No, it wasn't a tooth this time. I may as well tell you what it was," added Naomi, "since you're bound to know sooner or later. Well, then, Mr. Gilroy has left the station for good, and I am not ever going to marry him. That's all."

"And I'm thankful—"

Mrs. Potter checked herself with a gulp.

"So am I," said her mistress, dryly; "but it's a little exciting, and I let it keep me awake. You are to pack up his boxes, please, so that I may send them to the township in the spring-cart. But now make haste with the tea, for I need a cup badly, and I'll go and sing out to Mr. Engelhardt. Did you call him, by the way?"

"Yes, miss, I called him as usual."

Naomi left the breakfast-room, and was absent some three or four minutes. She came back looking somewhat scared.

"I've called him, too," she said, "at the top of my voice. But there's no making him hear anything. I've hammered at his door and at his window, too; both are shut, as if he wasn't up. I do wish that you would come and see whether he is."

A moment later Mrs. Potter was crossing the sandy yard, with Naomi almost treading on her ample skirts until they reached the barracks, which the elderly woman entered alone. No sooner, however, had she opened Engelhardt's door than she called her mistress to the spot. The room was empty. It was clear at a glance that the bed had not been slept in.

"If he hasn't gone away and left us without a word!" cried Mrs. Potter, indignantly.

"I am looking for his valise," said Naomi. "Where has he generally kept it?"

"Just there, underneath the dressing-table. He has taken it with him. There's nothing belonging to him in the room!"

"Except that half-crown under the tumbler, which is evidently meant for you. No, Mrs. Potter, I'm afraid you're right. The half-crown settles it. I should take it if I were you. And now I'll have my breakfast, if you please."

"But, miss, I can't understand—"

"No more can I. Make the tea at once, please. A little toast is all that I require with it."

And Naomi went slowly back toward the house, but stopped half way, with bent head and attentive eyes, and then went slower still. She had discovered in the sand the print of feet in stockings only. These tracks led up to the veranda, where they ended opposite the sitting-room door, which Naomi pushed open next moment. The room wore its ordinary appearance, but the pile of music which Engelhardt had brought with him for sale had been removed from the top of the piano to the music-stool; and lying conspicuously across the music, Naomi was mortified to find a silk handkerchief of her own, which the piano-tuner had worn all the week as a sling for his arm. She caught it up with an angry exclamation, and in doing so caught sight of some obviously left-handed writing on the topmost song of the pile. She stooped and read:

"These songs for Miss Pryse, with deep gratitude for all her kindness to Hermann Engelhardt."

It was a pale, set face that Mrs. Potter found awaiting her in the breakfast-room when the toast was ready and the tea made. Very little of the toast was eaten, and Mrs. Potter saw no more of her young mistress until the mid-day meal, to which Naomi sat down in her riding-habit.

"Just wait, Mrs. Potter," said she, hastily helping herself to a chop. "Take a chair yourself. I want to speak to you."

"Very good, miss," said the old lady, sitting down.

"I want to know when you last set eyes on Sam Rowntree."

"Let me see, miss. Oh, yes, I remember; it was about this time yesterday. He came to the kitchen, and told me he was going to run up a fresh mob of killing-sheep out of Top Scrubby, and how much meat could I do with? I said half a sheep, at the outside, and that was the last I saw of him."

"He never came near you last night?"

"That he didn't, miss. I was looking out for him. I wanted—"

"You didn't see him in the distance, or hear him whistling?"

"No, indeed I didn't."

"Well, he seems to have vanished into space," said Naomi, pushing away her plate and pouring out a cup of tea.

"It's too bad," said Mrs. Potter, with sympathy and indignation in equal parts. "I can't think what he means—to go and leave us alone like this."

"I can't think what Mr. Chester meant by not telling me that he was gone," remarked Naomi, hotly.

"I 'xpect he knew nothing about it, miss. He went off before daylight, him and the two men that come in with the sheep they was to take on to the shed."

"How can you know that?" inquired Naomi, with a touch of irritation. Her tea was very hot, and she was evidently in a desperate hurry.

"Because Mr. Chester asked me to put his breakfast ready for him overnight; and I did, too, and when I got up at six he'd had it and gone long ago. The teapot was cold. The men had gone, too, for I gave 'em their suppers last night, and they asked for a snack to take before their early start this morning. They must all have got away by five. They wouldn't hardly try to disturb Sam so early as all that; so they weren't to know he wasn't there."

"Well, he wasn't," said Naomi, "and it's disgraceful, that's what it is! Here we are without a man on the place, and there are nearly a hundred at the shed! I have had to catch a horse, and saddle it for myself." As she spoke Naomi made a last gulp at her hot tea, and then jumped up from the table.

"You are going to the shed, miss?"

"No; to the township."

"Ah, that's where you'll find him!"

"I hope I may," said Naomi, softly, and her eyes were far away. She was in the veranda, buttoning her gloves.

"I meant Sam Rowntree, miss."

Naomi blushed.

"I meant Mr. Engelhardt," said she, stoutly. "They are probably both there; but I have no doubt at all about Mr. Engelhardt. I am going to fetch the mail, but I hope I shall see that young gentleman, too, so that I may have an opportunity of telling him what I think of him."

"I should, miss, I should that!" cried Mrs. Potter, with virtuous wrath. "I should give him a piece of my mind about his way of treating them that's good and kind to him. I'm sure, miss, the notice you took of that young man—"

"Come, I don't think he's treated you so badly," interrupted Naomi, tartly. "Moreover, I am quite sure that he must have had some reason for going off so suddenly. I am curious to know what it was, and also what he expects me to do with his horse. If he had waited till this morning I would have sent him in with the buggy, and saved him a good old tramp. However, you don't mind being left in charge for an hour or so—eh, Mrs. Potter? No one ever troubles the homestead during shearing, you know."

"Oh, I shall be all right, miss, thank you," Mrs. Potter said, cheerfully; and she followed Naomi out into the yard, and watched her, in the distance, drag a box out of the saddle-room, mount from it, and set off at a canter toward the horse-paddock gate.

But Naomi did not canter all the way. She performed the greater part of her ride at a quiet amble, leaning forward in her saddle most of the time, and deciding what she should say to the piano-tuner, while she searched the ground narrowly for his tracks. She had the eagle eye for the trail of man or beast, which is the natural inheritance of all children of the bush. Before saddling the night-horse, she had made it her business to discover every print of a stocking sole that had been left about the premises during the night; and there were so many that she had now a pretty definite idea of the movements of her visitor prior to his final departure from the station. He had spent some time in aimless wandering about the moonlit yard. Then he had stood outside the kitchen, just where she had left him standing on the night of his arrival; and afterward had crossed the fence, just where they had crossed it together, and steered the very same course through the pines which she had led him that first evening. Still in his stockings, carrying his boots in his one hand and his valise under that arm (for she came to a place where he had dropped one boot, and, in picking it up, the valise also), he had worked round to the back veranda, and sat long on the edge, with his two feet in the soft sand, staring out over the scrub-covered, moonlit plain, just as he had sat staring many a time in broad daylight. Of all this Naomi was as certain as though she had seen it, because it was child's play to her to follow up the trail of his stockinged feet and to sort them out from all other tracks. But it ought to have been almost as easy to trace him in his boots on the well-beaten road to the township, and it was not.

The girl grew uncomfortable as she rode on and on without ever striking the trail; and the cutting sentences which she had prepared for the piano-tuner escaped her mind long before she reached the township, and found, as she now expected, that nobody answering to his description had been seen in the vicinity.

Naomi was not the one to waste time in a superfluity of inquiries. She saw in a moment that Engelhardt had not been near the place, and a similar fact was even more easily ascertained in the matter of Sam Rowntree. The township people knew him well. His blue fly-veil had not enlivened their hotel verandas for a whole week. So Naomi received her mail-bag and rode off without dismounting. A glimpse which she had caught of a red beard, at the other side of the broad sandy road, and the sound of a well-known voice shouting thickly, added to her haste. And on this journey she never once drew rein until her horse cantered into the long and sharp-cut shadows of the Taroomba stables.

As Naomi dismounted, Mrs. Potter emerged from the homestead veranda. The good woman had grown not a little nervous in her loneliness. Her looks as she came up were in striking contrast to those of her mistress. The one was visibly relieved; the other had come back ten times more anxious than she had gone away.

"No one been near you, Mrs. Potter?"

"Not a soul, miss. Oh, but it's good to see you back! I thought the afternoon was never coming to an end."

"They are neither of them at the township," said Naomi, with a miserable sigh.

"Nor have they been there at all—neither Mr. Engelhardt nor Sam Rowntree!"

Mrs. Potter cudgelled her poor brains for some—for any—kind of explanation.

"Sam did tell me"—she had begun, when she was promptly shut up.

"Who cares about Sam?" cried Naomi. "He's a good bushman; he can take care of himself. Besides, wherever he is, Sam isn't bushed. But anything may have happened to Mr. Engelhardt!"

"What do you think has happened?" the old lady asked, inanely.

"How am I to know?" was the wild answer. "I have nothing to go on. I know no more than you do."

Yet she stood thinking hard, with her horse still bridled and the reins between her fingers. She had taken off the saddle. Suddenly she slipped the reins over a hook and disappeared into the saddle-room. And in a few moments she was back, with a blanched face, and in her arms a packed valise.

"Is this Mr. Engelhardt's?"

Mrs. Potter took one look at it.

"It is," she said. "Yes, it is his!"

"Take it, then," said Naomi, mastering her voice with difficulty, "while I hunt up his saddle and bridle. If they are gone, all the better. Then I shall know he has his horse; and with a horse nothing much can happen to one."

She disappeared again, and was gone a little longer; but this time she came back desperately self-possessed.

"I have found his saddle. His bridle is not there at all. I know it's his saddle, because it's a pretty good one, and all our decent saddles are in use; besides, they all have the station brand upon them. This one has no brand at all. It must be Mr. Engelhardt's; and now I know exactly what he has done. Shall I tell you?"

Mrs. Potter clasped her hands.

"He has taken his bridle," said Naomi, still in a deadly calm, "and he has set out to catch his horse. How he could do such a thing I can't conceive! He knows the run of our horse-paddock no more than you do. He has failed to find his horse, tried to come back, and got over the fence into Top Scrubby. You don't know what that means! Top Scrubby's the worst paddock we have. It's half-full of mallee, it's six miles whichever way you take it, and the only drop of water in it is the tank at the township corner. Or he may be in the horse-paddock all the time. People who don't know the bush may walk round and round in a single square mile all day long, and until they drop. But it's no good our talking here; wherever he is, I mean to find him."

As she spoke she caught her saddle from the rail across which she had placed it, and was for flinging it on to her horse again, when Mrs. Potter interposed. The girl was trembling with excitement. The sun was fast sinking into the sand and scrub away west. In half an hour it would be dark.

"And no moon till ten or eleven," said Mrs. Potter, with sudden foresight and firmness. "You mustn't think of it, miss; you mustn't, indeed!"

"How can you say that? Why should you stop me? Do you mean me to leave the poor fellow to perish for want of water?"

"My dear, you could do no good in the dark," said Mrs. Potter, speaking as she had not spoken to Naomi since the latter was a little girl. "Besides, neither you nor the horse is fit for anything more until you've both had something to eat and drink."

"It's true!"

Naomi said this in helpless tones and with hopeless looks. As she spoke, however, her eyes fastened themselves upon the crimson ball just clear of the horizon, and all at once they filled with tears. Hardly conscious of what she did or said, she lifted up her arms and her voice to the sunset.

"Oh, my poor fellow! My poor boy! If only I knew where you were—if only I could see you now!"

CHAPTER XI

LOST IN THE BUSH

Had Naomi seen him then she would have found some difficulty in recognizing Hermann Engelhardt, the little piano-tuner whom already she seemed to have known all her life. Yet she had made a singularly shrewd guess at his whereabouts. Top Scrubby held him fast enough. And when Naomi stretched her arms toward the sunset, it is a strange fact that she also stretched them toward the lost young man, who was lying between it and her, not three miles from the spot on which she stood.

Within a mile of him ran the horse-paddock fence, which he had crossed by mistake at three o'clock that morning. He had never seen it again. All day he had wandered without striking track, or fence, or water. Once indeed his heart had danced at the sudden revelation of footprints under his very nose. They were crisp and clean and obviously recent. All at once they took a fatally familiar appearance. Slowly he lifted his right foot and compared the mark of it with the marks he had discovered. They were identical. To put the matter beyond a doubt he got both his feet into a couple of the old footprints. They fitted like pipes in a case. And then he knew that he was walking in circles, after the manner of lost men, and that he stood precisely where he had been three hours before.

That was a bitter moment. There were others and worse before sundown. The worst of all was about the time when Naomi flung out her arms and cried aloud in her trouble.

His staggering steps had brought him at last, near sundown, within sight of a ridge of pines which he seemed to know. The nearer he came to them the surer did he become that they were the station pines themselves. Footsore and faint and parched as he was, he plucked up all his remaining strength to reach those pines alive. If he were to drop down now it would be shameful, and he deserved to die. So he did not drop until he gained the ridge, and found the pines merely the outer ranks of a regular phalanx of mallee scrub. There was no mallee among the station pines. Nor would it have been possible to get so near to the homestead without squeezing through the wires of two fences at least. He had made a hideous and yet a fatuous mistake, and, when he realized it, he flung himself on his face in the shade of a hop-bush and burst into tears. To think that he must perish miserably after all, when, not five minutes since, he had felt the bottle-neck of the water-bag against his teeth—the smell of the wet canvas in his nostrils—the shrinking and lightening of the bag between his palms as the deep draught of cold water brought his dead throat to life.

It was all over now. He turned his face to the sand, and waited sullenly for the end. And presently a crow flew down from a pine, and hopped nearer and nearer to the prostrate body, with many a cautious pause, its wise black head now on one side, now on the other. Was it a dead body or a man asleep? There would have been no immediate knowing had not the crow been advancing between the setting sun and the man. Its shadow was a yard long when it came between Engelhardt's eyes, which were wide open, and the patch of sand that was warm with his breath. An instant later the crow was away with a hoarse scream, and Engelhardt was sitting up with a still hoarser oath upon his lips; indeed, he was inarticulate even to his own ears; but he found himself shaking his only fist at the crow, now a mere smut upon the evening sky, and next moment he was tottering to his feet.

He could hardly stand. His eyes were burning, his tongue swollen, his lips cracking like earth in a drought. He was aching, too, from head to foot, but he was not yet food for the crows. He set his teeth, and shook his head once or twice. Not yet—not yet.

The setting sun made a lane of light through the pines and mallee. The piano-tuner looked right and left along this lane, wondering which way to turn. He had no prejudice in the matter. All day he had been making calculations, and all day his calculations had been working out wrong. Like the struggles of a fly in a spider's web, each new effort left him more hopelessly entangled than the last. So now, without thinking, for thought was of no avail, he turned his face to the sunset, and, after half an hour's painful stumbling, was a mile farther from the station, and a mile deeper in the maze of Top Scrubby.

Night had fallen now, and the air was cool and sweet. This slightly refreshed him, and the continual chewing of leaves also did him some little good, as indeed it had done all day. But he was becoming troubled with a growing giddiness in addition to his other sufferings, and he well knew that the sands of his endurance were almost run. When the stars came out he once more altered his course, taking a new line by the Southern Cross; but it could not be for long, he was losing strength with every step. About this time it occurred to him to cut a branch for a staff, but when he took out his knife he was too weak to open the blade. A fatal lassitude was creeping over him. He could no longer think or even worry. Nothing mattered any more! Naomi—his mother—the plans and aspirations of his own life—they were all one to him now, and of little account even in the bulk. It had not been so a few hours earlier, but body and mind were failing together, and with no more hope there was but little more regret. His head and his heart grew light together, and when at last he determined to sit down and be done with it all, his greatest care was the choice of a soft and sandy place. It was as though he had been going to lie down for the night instead of for all time. And yet it was this, the mere fad of a wandering mind, that saved him; for before he had found what he wanted, suddenly—as by a miracle—he saw a light.

In a flash the man was alive and electrified. All the nerves in his body tightened like harp-strings, and the breath of life swept over them, leaving his heart singing of Naomi and his mother and the deeds to be done in this world. And the thrill remained; for the light was no phantom of a rocking brain, but a glorious reality that showed brighter and lighter every moment.

Yet it was a very long way off. He might never reach it at all. But he rushed on with never a look right or left, or up or down, as if his one chance of life lay in keeping his grip of that light steadfast and unrelaxed. His headlong course brought him twice to his knees with a thud that shook him to the very marrow. Once he ran his face into a tangle of small branches, and felt a hot stream flowing over his lips and chin; he sucked at it as it leapt his lips, and reeled on, thanking heaven that he could still see out of his eyes. The light had grown into a camp-fire, and he could hear men's voices around it. Their faces he could not see—only the leaping, crackling fire. He tried to coo-ee, but no sound would come. The thought crossed him that even now, within sight and ear-shot of his fellow-men, he might drop for good. His heart kept throbbing against his ribs like an egg boiling in a pan, and his every breath was as a man's last gasp. He passed some horses tethered among the trees. Then before the fire there stood a stout figure with shaded eyes and pistols in his belt; another joined him; then a third, with a rifle; and the three loomed larger with every stride, until Engelhardt fell sprawling and panting in their midst, his hat gone, his long hair matted upon his forehead, and the white face beneath all streaming with sweat and blood.

"By God, he's dying!" said one of the men, flinging away his fire-arm. "Yank us the water-bag, mate, and give the cuss a chance."

Engelhardt looked up, and saw one of his two enemies, the swagmen, reaching out his hand for the bag. It was the smaller and quieter of the pair—the man with the weather-beaten face and the twinkling eye—and as Engelhardt looked further he saw none other than Simons, the discharged shearer, handing the dripping bag across. But a third hand stretched over and snatched it away with a bellowing curse.

"What a blessed soft pair you are! Can't you see who 'e is? It's 'is bloomin' little nibs with the broke arm, and not a damned drop does he get from me!"

"Come on, Bill," said the other tramp. "Why not?"

"He knows why not," said Bill, who, of course, was the stout scoundrel with the squint. "Don't you, sonny?" And he kicked Engelhardt in the side with his flat foot.

"Easy, mate, easy. The beggar's dying!"

"All the better! If he don't look slippy about it I'll take an' slit his throat for him!"

"Well, give him a drop o' water first."

"Ay, give 'im a drink, whether or no," put in Simons. "No tortures, mate! The plain thing's good enough for me."

"And me, too!"

"Why, Bo's'n," cried Bill, "you've got no more spunk than a blessed old ewe! You sailors and shearers are plucky fine chaps to go mates with in a job like ours! You wouldn't have done for poor old Tigerskin!"

"To hell with Tigerskin," said Simons, savagely. "We've heard more than enough of him. Give the beggar a drink, or, by cripes, I'm off it!"

"All right, boys, all right. You needn't get so scotty about it, matey. But he sha'n't drink more than's good for 'im, and he sha'n't drink much at a time, or 'e'll burst 'is skin!"

As he spoke Bill uncorked the water-bag, hollowed a filthy palm, flooded it, and held it out to the piano-tuner, who all this time had been sitting still and listening without a word.

"Drink out o' my hand," said he, "or not at all."

But Engelhardt could only stare at the great hairy paw thrust under his nose. It had no little finger. He was trying to remember what this meant.

"Drink out o' that, you swine," thundered Bill, "and be damned to you!"

Human nature could endure no more. Instead of drinking, Engelhardt knocked the man's hand up, and made a sudden grab at the water-bag. He got it, too, and had swallowed a mouthful before it was plucked away from him. The oaths came pouring out of Bill's mouth like sheep racing through a gate. But the piano-tuner had tasted what was more to him than blood, and he made a second dash at the bag, which resulted in a quantity of water being spilled; so without struggling any more, he fell upon his face with his lips to the wet sand.

"Let the joker suck," said Bill; "I'll back the sand!"

But Engelhardt rolled over on his left side and moved no more.

Simons knelt over him.

"He's a stiff 'un, mates. My blessed oath he is! That's number two, an' both on 'em yours, Bill."

Bill laughed.

"That'll be all right," said he. "Where's my pipe got to? I'm weakenin' for a smoke."

CHAPTER XII

FALLEN AMONG THIEVES

There was life in Engelhardt yet, though for some time he lay as good as dead. The thing that revived him was the name of Naomi Pryse on the lips of the late ringer of the Taroomba shed. The piano-tuner listened for more without daring to open his eyes or to move a muscle. And more came with a horrifying flow of foul words.

"She had the lip to sack me! But I'll be even with her before the night's out. Yes, by cripes, by sunrise she'll wish she'd never been born!"

"It's not the girl we're after," said Bill's voice, with a pause and a spit. "It's the silver." And Engelhardt could hear him puffing at his pipe.

"It's gold and silver. She's the gold."

"I didn't dislike her," said the sailor-man. "I'd leave her be."

"She didn't sack you from the shed. Twelve pound a week it meant, with that image over the board!"

"Bo's'n'd let the whole thing be, I do believe," said Bill, "if we give 'im 'alf a chance."

"Not me," said Bo's'n. "I'll stick to my messmates. But we've stiffened two people already. It's two too many."

"What about your skipper down at Sandridge?"

"Well, I reckon he's a stiff 'un, too."

"Then none o' your skite, mate," said Bill, knocking out a clay pipe against his heel. "Look ye here, lads; it's a blessed Providence that's raked us together, us three. Here's me, straight out o' quod, coming back like a bird to the place where there's a good thing on. Here's Bo's'n, he's bashed in his skipper's skull and cut and run for it. We meet and we pal on. The likeliest pair in the Colony! And here's old Simons, knocked cock-eye by this 'ere gal, and swearing revenge by all that's bloody. He has a couple of horses, too—just the very thing we wanted—so he's our man. Is he on? He is. Do we join hands an' cuss an' swear to see each other through? We do—all three. Don't we go to the township for a few little necessaries an' have a drink on the whole thing? We do. Stop a bit! Doesn't a chap and a horse come our way, first shot off? Don't we want another horse, an' take it, too, ay and cook that chap's hash in fit an' proper style? Of course we do. Then what's the good o' talking? Tigerskin used to say, 'We'll swing together, matey, or by God we'll drive together in a coach-and-four with yeller panels and half-a-dozen beggars in gold lace and powdered wigs.' So that's what I say to you. There's that silver. We'll have it and clear out with it at any blessed price. We've let out some blood already. A four-hundred-gallon tankful more or less can make no difference now. We can only swing once. So drink up, boys, and make your rotten lives happy while you have 'em. There's only one thing to settle: whether do we start at eleven, or twelve, or one in the morning?"

Engelhardt heard a pannikin passed round and sucked at by all three. Then a match was struck and a pipe lit. His veins were frozen; he was past a tremor.

"Eleven's too early," said Simons; "it's getting on for ten already. I'm for a spell before we start; there's nothing like a spell to steady your nerve."

"I'd make it eight bells—if not seven," argued the Bo's'n. "The moon'll be up directly. The lower she is when we start, the better for us. You said the station lay due east, didn't you, Bill? Then it'll be easy steering with a low moon."

The other two laughed.

"These 'ere sailors," said Bill, "they're a blessed treat. Always in such an almighty funk of getting bushed. I've known dozens, and they're all alike."

"There's no fun in it," said the Bo's'n. "Look at this poor devil."

Engelhardt held his breath.

"I suppose he is corpsed?" said Bill.

"Dead as junk."

"Well, he's saved us the trouble. I'd have stuck the beggar as soon as I'd stick a sheep. There's only one more point, lads. Do we knock up her ladyship, and make her let us into the store—"

"Lug her out by her hair," suggested Simons. "I'll do that part."

"Or do we smash into it for ourselves? That's the game Tigerskin an' me tried, ten years ago. It wasn't good enough. You know how it panned out. Still, we ain't got old Pryse to reckon with now. He was a terror, he was! So what do you say, boys? Show hands for sticking-up—and now for breaking in. Then that settles it."

Engelhardt never knew which way it was settled.

"The she-devil!" said Simons. "The little snake! I can see her now, when she come along the board and sang out for the tar-boy all on her own account. That little deader, there, he was with her. By cripes, if she isn't dead herself by morning she'll wish she was! I wonder how she'll look to-night? Not that way, by cripes, that's one thing sure! You leave her to me, mates! I shall enjoy that part. She sha'n't die, because that's what she'd like best; but she shall apologize to me under my own conditions—you wait and see what they are. They'll make you smile. The little devil! Twelve pound a week! By cripes, but I'll make her wish she was as dead as her friend here. I'll teach her—"

"Stiffen me purple," roared Bill, "if the joker's not alive after all!"

The rogues were sitting round their fire in a triangle, Simons with his back to the supposed corpse; when he looked over his shoulder, there was his dead man glaring at him with eyes like blots of ink on blood-stained paper.

Engelhardt, in fact, had been physically unable to lie still any longer and hear Naomi so foully threatened and abused. But the moment he sat up he saw his folly, and tried, quick as thought, to balance it by gaping repeatedly in Simons's face.

"I beg your pardon, I'm sure," said he, in the civilest manner. "I'd been asleep, and couldn't think where I was. I assure you I hadn't the least intention of interrupting you."

His voice was still terribly husky. Bill seized the water-bag and stuck it ostentatiously between his knees. Simons only scowled.

"Please go on with what you were saying," said Engelhardt, crawling to the fire and sitting down between these two worthies. "All I ask is a drink and a crust. I've been out all day without bite or sup. Yes, and all last night as well! That's all I ask. I am dead tired. I'd sleep like a stone."

No one spoke, but presently, without a word, Bill took a pannikin, filled it from the water-bag, and sullenly handed it to the piano-tuner. Then he knifed a great wedge from a damper and tossed it across. Engelhardt could scarcely believe his eyes, so silently, so unexpectedly was it done. He thanked the fellow with unnecessary warmth, but no sort of notice was taken of his remarks. He was half afraid to touch without express permission the water which he needed so sorely. He even hesitated, pannikin in hand, as he looked from one man to the other; but the villanous trio merely stared at him with fixed eyeballs, and at last he raised it to his lips and swallowed a pint at one draught.

Even the mouthful he had fought for earlier in the evening—even that drop had sent a fresh stream of vitality swimming through his veins. But this generous draught made a new man of him in ten seconds. He wanted more, it is true; but the need was now a mere desire; and then there was the damper under his eyes. He never knew how hungry he was until he had quenched his thirst and started to eat. Until he had finished the slice of damper, he took no more heed of his companions than a dog with a bone. Bill threw him a second wedge, and this also he devoured without looking up. But his great thirst had never been properly slaked, and the treatment he was now receiving emboldened him to hold out the pannikin for more water. Even this was granted him, but still without a word. Since he had arisen and joined them by the fire, not one of the men had addressed a single remark to him, and his own timid expressions of thanks and attempts at affability had been received all alike in impenetrable silence. Nor were the ruffians talking among themselves. They just sat round the fire, their rough faces reddened by the glow, their weapons scintillating in the light, and stared fixedly at the little man who had stumbled among them. Their steady taciturnity soon became as bad to bear as the conversation he had overheard while feigning insensibility. There was a kind of sinister contemplation in their looks which was vague, intangible, terrifying. Then their vile plot ringing in his ears, with dark allusions to a crime already committed, made the piano-tuner's position sickening, intolerable. He spoke again, and again received no answer. He announced that he was extremely grateful to them for saving his life, but that he must now push on to the township. They said nothing to this. He wished them good-night; they said nothing to that. Then he got to his feet, and found himself on the ground again quicker than he had risen. Bill had grabbed him by the ankle, still without a syllable. When Engelhardt looked at him, however, the heavy face and squinting eyes met him with a series of grimaces, so grotesque, so obscene, that he was driven to bury his face in his one free hand, and patiently to await his captors' will. He heard the Bo's'n chuckling; but for hours, as it seemed to him, that was all.

"Who is the joker?" said Bill, at last. "What does he do for his rations?"

"They say as 'e tunes pianners," said Simons.

"Then he don't hang out on Taroomba?"

"No; 'e only come the other day, an' goes an' breaks his arm off a buck-jumper. So they were saying at the shed."

"Well, he enjoyed his supper, didn't he? It's good to see 'em enjoying theirselves when their time is near. Boys, you was right; it would have been a sin to send 'im to 'ell with an empty belly an' a sandy throat. If ever I come to swing, I'll swing with a warm meal in my innards, my oath!"

Engelhardt held up his head.

"So you mean to kill me, do you?" said he, very calmly, but with a kind of scornful indignation. Bill gave him a horrible leer, but no answer.

"I suppose there's nothink else for it," said Simons, half-regretfully; "though mark you, mates, I'm none so keen on the kind o' game."

"No more ain't I," cried the Bo's'n, with vigor. "I'd give the cove a chance, Bill."

"How?" said Bill.

"I'd lash the beggar to a tree and leave him to snuff out for hisself."

Engelhardt laughed aloud in mock gratitude.

"Oh, I ain't partickler as to ways," said Bill. "One way's as good as another for me. There's no bloomin' 'urry, any'ow. The moon ain't up yet, and before we go this beggar's got to tell us things. He heard what we was saying, mates. I seen it in his eye. Didn't you, you swine?"

Engelhardt took no kind of notice.

"Didn't you—you son of a mangy bandicoot?"

Still Engelhardt would have held his tongue; but Bill started kicking him on one side, and Simons on the other; and the pain evoked an answer in a note of shrill defiance.

"I did!" he cried. "I heard every word."

"We're after that silver."

"I know you are."

"You've seen it?"

"I have."

"Tell us all about it."

"Not I!"

For this he got a kick on each side.

"Is it in the store yet?"

No answer.

"Is the chest easy to find?"

No answer.

"Is it covered up?"

"Or underground?"

"Or made to look like something else?"

Each man contributed a question; none elicited a word; no more did their boots; it was no use kicking him.

There was a long pause. Then Bill said:

"You've lost your hat. You need another. Here you are."

He had blundered to his feet, stepped aside out of the ring of light, and spun a wide-awake into Engelhardt's lap. He started. It was adorned with a blue silk fly-veil.

"Recognize it?"

He had recognized it at once; it was Sam Rowntree's; and Sam Rowntree had been missing, yesterday, before Engelhardt himself said his secret farewell to the homestead.

He looked for more. No more was said. The villains had relapsed into that silence which was more eloquent of horror than all their threats. But Bill now flung fresh branches on the fire; the wood crackled; the flames spurted starward; and in the trebled light, Engelhardt, peering among the trees for some further sign of Sam, saw that which set the pores pringling all over his skin.

It was the glint of firelight upon a pair of spurs that hung motionless in the scrub—not a yard from the ground—not ten paces from the fire.

He looked again; the spurs were fixed to a pair of sidespring boots; the boots hung out of a pair of moleskins, with a few inches of worsted sock in between. All were steady, immovable as the stars above. He could see no higher than the knees; but that was enough; a hoarse cry escaped him, as he pointed with a quivering finger, and turned his white face from man to man.

Neither Simons nor the Bo's'n would meet his look; but Bill gripped his arm, with a loud laugh, and dragged him to his feet.

"Come and have a look at him," he said. "He isn't pretty, but he'll do you good."

Next instant Engelhardt stood close to the suspended body of the unfortunate Rowntree. Both hands were tied behind his back, his hair was in his eyes, and the chin drooped forward upon his chest like that of a man lost in thought.

"See what you'll come to," said Bill, giving the body a push that set it swinging like a pendulum, while the branch creaked horribly overhead. "See what you'll come to if you don't speak out! It was a good ten minutes before he stopped kicking and jingling his spurs; you're lighter, and it'd take you longer. Quarter of an hour, I guess, or twenty minutes."

Engelhardt had reeled, and would have fallen, but the Bo's'n jumped up and caught him in his arms.

He did more.

"Listen to reason, messmate," said the sailor, with a touch of rude friendliness in his lowered tone. "There ain't no sense in keeping mum with us. If you won't speak, you'll swing at the yard-arm along with t'other cove in a brace of shakes; if you will, you'll get a chance whether or no. Besides, what good do you think you can do? We know all that's worth knowing. Anything you tell us'll make less trouble in at the homestead—not more."

"All right," said Engelhardt, faintly. "Let me sit down; I'll tell you anything you like."

"That's more like. Take my place, then you'll be stern-on to that poor devil. Now then, Bill, fire away. The little man's hisself again."

"Good for him," growled Bill. "Look at me, you stuck pig, and answer questions. Where's that chest?"

"In the store."

"Didn't I say so! Never been shifted! Whereabouts in the store?"

"Inside the counter."

"Much of a chest to bust into?"

"Two locks, and clamps all over."

"Where's the keys?"

"I don't know. Miss Pryse keeps them."

"She won't keep 'em long. See here, you devil, if you look at me again like that I'll plug your eyes into your mouth! You seem to know a fat lot about this silver. Have you seen it, or haven't you?"

"I have."

"What is there?"

"Not much. A couple of candlesticks; a few spoons; some old skewers; a biscuit-box; a coffee-pot—but it's half ivory; an epergne—"

"What the 'ells that? None o' your Greek, you swine!"

"It's a thing for flowers."

"Why didn't you say so, then? What else?"

"Let me see—"

"You'd best look slippy!"

"Well, there's not much more. A cake-basket, some napkin-rings, and a pair of nut-crackers. And that's about all. It's all I saw, anyhow."

"All silver?"

"I shouldn't think it."

"You liar! You plucky well know it is. And not a bad lot neither, even if it was the lot. By the Lord, I've a good mind to strip and sit you on that fire for not telling me the truth!"

"Easy, mate, easy!" remonstrated the Bo's'n. "That sounds near enough."

"By cripes," cried Simons, "it's near enough for me. 'Tain't the silver I want. It's the gold, and that's the girl!"

"You won't get her," said Engelhardt.

"Why not?"

"She'll put a bullet through you."

"Can she shoot straight?"

"As straight as her father, I should say. I never saw him. But I've seen her."

"What do?"

"Stand in the veranda and knock a crow off the well fence—with her own revolver."

"By cripes, that's a lie."

(It was.)

"I'm not so blooming sure," said Bill. "I recollect how the old man dropped Tigerskin at nigh twenty yards. She was with him, too, at the time—a kid out of bed. I took a shot at her and missed. She'd be as likely as not to knock a hole through one or other of us, lads, if you hadn't got me to see you through. You trust to Bill for ideas! He's got one now, but it'll keep. See here, you swine, you! When was it you saw all what you pretend to have seen, eh?"

Engelhardt laughed. His answer could do no harm, and it gave him a thrill of satisfaction to score even so paltry a point against his bestial antagonist.

"It was the day you two came around the station."

"That morning?"

"Yes."

"Where did you see it?"

"In the store."

"Before we came?"

"While you were there. When Miss Pryse locked the door, it was all over the place. While we were in the kitchen she got it swept out of sight."

"Good God!" screamed Bill; "if only I'd known. You little devil, if only I'd guessed it!"

His vile face was convulsed and distorted with greed and rage; his hairy, four-fingered fist shaking savagely in Engelhardt's face. Bo's'n remonstrated again.

"What's the sense o' that, messmate? For God's sake shut it! A fat lot we could ha' done without a horse between us."

"We could have rushed the store, stretched 'em stiff—"

"And carried a hundredweight o' silver away in our bluies! No, no, my hearty; it's a darn sight better as it is. What do you say, Simons?"

"I'm glad you waited, but I'm bleedin' dry."

"An' me, too," said Bill, sulkily, as he uncorked a black bottle. "Give us that pannikin, you spawn!"

Engelhardt handed it over unmoved. He was past caring what was said or done to him personally. Bill drank first.

"Here's fun!" said he, saluting the other two simultaneously with a single cross-eyed leer.

"'An' they say so—an' we hope so!'" chanted the Bo's'n, who came next. "Anyway, here's to the moon, for there she spouts!"

As he raised his pannikin, he pointed it over Engelhardt's shoulder, and the latter involuntarily turned his head. He brought it back next moment, with a jerk and a shudder. Far away, behind the scrub, on the edge of the earth, lay the moon, with a silvery pathway leading up to her, and a million twigs and branches furrowing her face. But against the top of the great white disc there fell those horrible boots and spurs, in grisly silhouette, and still swaying a little to the mournful accompaniment of the groaning bough above. Surely the works of God and man were never in ghastlier contrast than when Engelhardt turned his head without thinking and twitched it back with a shudder. And yet to him this was not the worst; he was now in time to catch that which made the blood run colder still in all his veins.

CHAPTER XIII

A SMOKING CONCERT

Simons was toasting Naomi Pryse. It took Engelhardt some moments to realize this. The language he could stand; but no sooner did he grasp its incredible application than his self-control boiled over on the spot.

"Stop it!" he shrieked at the shearer. "How dare you speak of her like that? How dare you?"

The foul mouth fell open, and the camp-fire flames licked the yellow teeth within. Engelhardt was within a few inches of them, with a doubled fist and reckless eyes. To his amazement, the man burst out laughing in his face.

"The little cuss has spunk," said he. "I like to see a cove stick up for 'is gal, by cripes I do!"

"So do I," said Bo's'n. "Brayvo, little man, brayvo!"

"My oath," said Bill, "I'd have cut 'is stinkin' throat for 'alf as much if I'd been you, matey!"

"Not me," said Simons. "I'll give 'im a drink for 'is spunk. 'Ere, kiddy, you wish us luck!"

He held out the pannikin. Engelhardt shook his head. He was, in fact, a teetotaler, who had made a covenant with himself, when sailing from old England, to let no stimulant pass his lips until his feet should touch her shores again. The covenant was absolutely private and informal, as between a man and his own body, but no power on earth would have made him break it.

"Come on," said Simons. "By cripes, we take no refusals here!"

"I must ask you to take mine, nevertheless."

"Why?"

"Because I don't drink."

"Well, you've got to!"

"I shall not!"

Simons seemed bent upon it. Perhaps he had taken a drop too much himself; indeed, none of the three were entirely above such a suspicion; but it immediately appeared that this small point was to create more trouble than everything that had gone before. Small as it was, neither man would budge an inch. Engelhardt said again that he would not drink. Simons swore that he should either drink or die. The piano-tuner cheerfully replied that he expected to die in any case, but he wasn't going to touch whiskey for anybody; so he gave Simons leave to do what he liked and get it over—the sooner the better. The shearer promptly seized him by his uninjured wrist, twisted it violently behind his back, and held out his hand to Bo's'n for the pannikin. Engelhardt was now helpless, his left arm a prisoner and in torture, his right lying useless in a sling. Bo's'n, however, came to his rescue once more, by refusing to see good grog wasted when there was little enough left.

"What's the use?" said he. "If the silly devil won't drink, we'll make him sing us a song. He says he tunes pianners. Let him tune up now!"

"That's better," assented Bill. "The joker shall give us a song before we let his gas out; and I'll drink his grog. Give it here, Bo's'n."

The worst of a gang of three is the strong working majority always obtainable against one or other of them. Simons gave in with a curse, and sent Engelhardt sprawling with a heavy kick. As he picked himself up, they called upon him to sing. He savagely refused.

"All right," said Bill, "we'll string him up an' be done with him. I'm fairly sick o' the swine—I am so!"

"By cripes, so am I."

"Then up he goes."

"The other beggar's got the rope," said Bo's'n.

"Then cut him down. He won't improve by hanging any longer. We ain't a-going to eat him, are we? Cut him down, and sling this one up. It's your job, Bo's'n."

Bo's'n was disposed to grumble. Bill cut him short.

"All right," said he, getting clumsily to his feet, "I'll do it myself. You call yourself a bloomin' man! I'd make a better bloomin' man than you with bloomin' baccy-ash. Out of the light, you cripple, an' the thing'll be done in half the time you take talking about it!"

Engelhardt was left sitting between Simons and the ill-used Bo's'n. The latter had his grumble out, but Bill took no more account of him. As for the shearer, the ferocity of his attitude toward the doomed youth was now second to none. He sat very close to him, with a hellish scowl and a great hand held ready to blast any attempt at escape. But none was made. The piano-tuner stuck his thumbs into his ears, covered his closed eyes with his palms, and tried both to think and to pray. He could not think; vague visions of Naomi crowded his mind, but they formed no thought. Nor could he pray for anything but courage to meet his fate. Within a few yards of him was the body of a dead man murdered by these thieves among whom he himself had fallen. He could not but doubt that they were about to murder him too. His last hour had come. He wanted courage. That was all he asked for as he sat with plugged ears and tight-shut eyes.

He was aroused by a smart kick in the ribs. As he got up to go to his doom, Bill seized him by the shoulders and pushed him roughly toward the hanging rope; it hung so low, it bisected the rising moon.

"Let me alone," he cried, wriggling fiercely. "I can get there without your help."

"Well, we'll see."

He got there fast enough. A little deeper in the scrub he could see a shapeless mass of moleskin and Crimean shirting, with a spurred boot half covered by a stiff hand. He was thankful to turn his face to the blazing camp-fire, even though the noose went round his neck as he did so.

"Now then," said Bill, hauling the rope taut, "will you give us a song or won't you?"

He could not speak.

"If you sing us a song we may give you another hour," said the Bo's'n from the ground. Simons and he had been whispering together. Bill shook his head at them.

"That rests with me," said he to Engelhardt. "Don't you make any mistake."

"Another hour!" cried the young man, bitterly, as he found his voice. "What's another hour? If you're men at all, put an end to me now and be done with it."

"How's that?" said Bill, hauling him upon tip-toe. "No, no, sonny, we want our song first," he added, as he let the rope fall slack again.

"Sing up, and there's no saying what'll happen," cried the Bo's'n, cheerily.

"What shall I sing?"

"Anything you like."

"Something funny to cheer us up."

"Ay, ay, a comic song!"

Engelhardt wavered—as once before under the eyes and ears of a male audience. "I'll do my best," he said at last. And Bo's'n clapped.

A minute later the bushrangers' camp was the scene of as queer a performance as ever was given. A very young man, with a pallid, blood-stained face, and a rope round his neck, was singing a "comic" song to a parcel of cut-throats who were presently to hang him, as they had hanged already the corpse at his heels. Meanwhile they surrendered themselves like simple innocents to a thorough enjoyment of the fine fun provided. The replenished camp-fire lit their villanous faces with a rich red glow. They grinned, they laughed, they displayed their pleasure and satisfaction each after his own fashion. The fat man shook in his fat; the long man showed his grinning teeth; the sailor-man slapped his thighs and rolled on the ground in paroxysms of spirituous mirth. It must have been the humor of the situation, rather than that of the song, which so powerfully appealed to them. The former had the piquant charm of being entirely their own creation. The latter was that poetic paraphrase of the early chapters of the Book of Genesis which the singer had tried upon another back-block audience but a few nights before. Of the two, this audience, as such, was decidedly the better. At any rate they let him get to the end. And when that came, and Bo's'n clapped again, even the other two joined in the applause.

"By cripes," said Simons, "that's not so bad!"

"Bad?" cried the enthusiastic Bo's'n. "It's as good as fifty plays. We'll have some more, and I'll give you a song myself."

"Right!" said Bill. "The night's still young. Stiffin me purple if we haven't forgot them weeds we laid in at the township! Out with 'em, mateys, an' pass round the grog; we'll make a smokin' concert of it. A bloomin' smoker, so help me never!"

The cigars were unearthed from the pockets of Bill himself. He and Simons at once put two of them in full blast. Meantime, Bo's'n was trying his voice.

"Any of you know any sailors' chanties?" said he.

A pause, and then—

"Yes, I do."

The voice was none other than Engelhardt's.

"You? The devil you do! How's that, then?"

"I came out in a sailing ship."

"What do you know?"

"Some of the choruses."

"'Blow the land down?'"

"Yes—best of all."

"Then we'll have that! Messmates you join his nibs in the chorus. I sing yarn and chorus too. Ready? Steady! Here goes!"

And in a rich, rolling voice, that had been heard above many a gale on the high seas, he began with the familiar words:

Oh, where are you going to, my pretty maid?—
Yo-ho, blow the land down!
Oh, where are you going to, my pretty maid?—
And give us some time to blow the land down!

The words were not long familiar. They quickly became detestable. The farther they went, of course, the more they appealed to Simons, Bill, and the singer himself. As for Engelhardt, obviously he was in no position to protest; nor could mere vileness add at all to his discomfort, with that noose still round his neck, and the rope-end still tight in Bill's clutch. Then the refrain for every other line was no bad thing in itself; at all events, he joined in throughout, and at the close stood at least as well with his persecutors as before.

It now appeared, however, that sailors' chanties were the Bo's'n's weakness. He insisted on singing two more, with topical and impromptu verses of his own. As, for instance:

The proud Miss Pryse may toss 'er 'ead—
An' they say so—an' we hope so—
The proud Miss Pryse will soon be dead—
The poor—old—gal!

Or again, and as bad:

Oh, they call me Hanging Johnny—
Hurray! Pull away!
An' I'll soon hang you, my sonny—
Hang—boys—hang!

These are but opening verses. There were many more in each case, and they were bad enough in all respects. And yet Engelhardt chimed in at his own expense—even at Naomi's—because it might be that his life and hers depended upon it. He was beginning to have his hopes, partly from the delay, partly from looks and winks which he had seen exchanged; and his hopes led to ideas, because his brain had never been clearer and busier than it was now become. He was devoutly thankful not to have been twice forced to sing. The second time, however, was still to come. It was announced by a jerk of the rope that went near to dislocating his neck.

"This image is doing nothink for 'is living, an' yet we're letting 'im live!" cried Bill, in a tone of injured and abused magnanimity. "Sing, you swine, or swing! One o' the two."

"What sort will you have this time?" asked Engelhardt, meekly. His meekness was largely put on, however. The black bottle had been going round pretty freely; in fact, it was quite empty. Another had been broached, and the men were both visibly and audibly in their cups.

"Another comic!" cried Simons and the Bo's'n in one breath.

"No, something serious this trip," Bill said, contradictiously. "You know warri mean, you lubber—somethin' soothin' for a night-cap—somethin' Christy-mental. Go ahead an' be damned to ye!"

Engelhardt had no time to consider, to reflect, to choose. The signal to start instantly was given by a series of sharp, throttling jerks at the rope. Almost before he was himself aware of it, he was giving them the well-known "Swannee River." It was the first "Christy-mental" song that had risen to his mind and lips. Moreover, he gave it with all the pathos and expression of which he was capable, and that, as we know, was not inconsiderable. They did not join in the chorus. This made it the easier. He tried to forget that these men were there, and, throwing his gaze aloft, sung softly—even sweetly—to the stars. Doubtless it was all acting, and by a cunning instinct that he went so slow in the final chorus:

Oh, my heart is sad and weary,
Everywhere I roam;
Oh, darkies, but my heart is weary,
Far from the old folks at home.

And yet one knows that it is possible to act and to feel at one and the same time; and, incredible as it may seem in the circumstances, Engelhardt found it so just then. He did think of the dear old woman at home; and being an artist to his boots, he gave his emotions their head, and sang to these blackguards as he would have sung to Naomi herself. And the effect was extraordinary—if in part due to the whiskey. When the young man lowered his eyes there was the maudlin Bo's'n snivelling like a babe, and the other two sucking their cigars to life with faces as long as lanterns.

"Lads," said Bill, "the night's still young. What matter does it make when we tackle the station? It'll keep. We on'y got to get there before mornin'. 'Tain't midnight yet." His voice was thickish.

"If the moon gets much higher," hiccoughed the Bo's'n, "we'll never get there at all. We'll never find it!" And he dried his eyes on his sleeve.

Bill took no notice of this. But he shook up his companions, linked arms between the two, and halted them in front of Engelhardt. They all three swayed a little as they stood, yet all three were still dangerously sober; and the second bottle was empty now; and there was no third. Engelhardt confronted them with hope, but not confidence, and listened, more eagerly than he dared to show, to Bill's harangue.

"Young man," said he, "you're not such a cussed swine's I thought. Sing or swing, says I. You sings like a man. So you sha'n't swing at all—not yet. No saying what we'll do in an hour or two. P'r'aps we're going to take you along with us to the station, to show us things, an' p'r'aps we ain't. You make your miseral life happy, to go on with. You bloomin' beggar, you, we respite you! Bo's'n, take the same rope an' lash the joker to that tree."

Bill stopped to see it done. He was quite sober enough to be sufficiently particular in this matter; as was Bo's'n, to perform his part in sailor-like fashion. In five minutes the thing was done.

"What do you think of that?" cried the seaman, with a certain honest sort of deep-sea pride.

"It'll do, matey."

"By cripes, he'll never get out of that!"

In fact, from his chin to his knees, the poor piano-tuner was encased in a straight-waistcoat of rope—the rope that had been round his neck for the last half-hour. Even the injured arm was inside. Nor could he move his feet, for they were tied separately at the ankles. Otherwise there was only one knot in what was indeed a masterpiece of its kind.

"I hope you'll be comfortable," said the Bo's'n, with a quaint touch of remorse, "for split me if you didn't sing like a blessed cock-angel! And never you fear," he added, under his breath, "for we ain't agoin' to hang you. Not us! And if there's anything we can do for you afore we take our spell, say the word, messmate, say the word."

The piano-tuner shook his head.

"Then so long and—"

"Stop! you might give us a cigar."

It was given readily.

"Thanks; and now you might light it."

This also was done, with a brand from the dying fire.

"Good-night," said Bo's'n.

"And thank you," added Engelhardt.

The sailor stopped to give a last admiring glance at his handiwork; then he joined his companions, who were already spread out upon the broad of their backs; and Engelhardt was left to himself at last— unable to move hand or foot—with a corpse at hand and the murderers under his eyes—with the risen moon shining full upon his face, and the vilest of vile cigars held tight between his teeth.

And he was no smoker; tobacco made him sick.

Nevertheless, he kept that bad weed alight, and very carefully alight, for ten minutes by guess-work. Then he depressed his chin, knocked off an inch of ash against the top-most coil, applied the red end to the rope, and sucked and puffed for his life and Naomi's.

CHAPTER XIV

THE RAID ON THE STATION

Those same dark hours of this eventful night were also the slowest and the dreariest on record in the mind of Naomi Pryse. She too had waited for the moon. At sundown she had stabled her horse, and left it with a fine feed of chaff and oats as priming for the further work she had in view. This done, she had consented, under protest, to eat something herself; but had jumped up early to fill with her own hands a water-bag and a flask of which she could have no need for hours. It made no matter. She must be up and doing this or that; it was intolerable sitting still even to eat and drink. Besides, how could she eat, how could she drink, when he who should have shared her meal was perhaps perishing of hunger and thirst in Top Scrubby? It was much more comforting to cut substantial slices of mutton and bread, to put them up in a neat packet, and to set this in readiness alongside the flask and the water-bag. Then came the trouble. There was nothing more to be done.

It was barely eight o'clock, and no moon for two hours and a half.

Naomi went round to the back veranda, picked up the book she had been reading the day before, and marched about with it under her arm. She had not the heart to sit down and read. Her restless feet took her many times to the kitchen and Mrs. Potter, who shook her good gray head and remonstrated with increasing candor and asperity.

"Go to look for him?" she cried at last. "When the time comes for that, you'll be too dead tired to sit in your saddle, miss. If you start before the moon's well up, there'll be no telling a hoof-mark from a foot-print without getting off every time. You've said so yourself, Miss Naomi. Then why not go straight to your bed and lie down for two or three hours? I'll bring you a cup of tea at half-past eleven, and you can be away by twelve."

Naomi sighed.

"It is so long to wait—doing nothing! He may be dying, poor fellow; and yet what can one do in the dark?"

"Lie down and rest," said Mrs. Potter, dryly.

"Well, I will try, but not on my bed—on the sitting-room sofa, I think. Will you light the lamp there, please? And bring the tea at eleven; I'll start at half-past."

Naomi took a short stroll among the darkling pines—the way that she had taken the piano-tuner in the first moments of their swift friendship—the way that he had taken alone last night. She reached the sitting-room with moist, wistful eyes, which startled themselves as she confronted the mirror over the chimney-piece whereon stood the lamp. She stood for a little, however, looking at herself—steadfastly—inquisitively—as though to search out the secrets of her own heart. She gave it up in the end, and turned wearily away. What was the use of peering into her own heart now, when so often aforetime she had seemed to know it, and had not? There was no use; and as it happened, no need. For the first thing her eyes fell upon, as she turned, was the pile of music lying yet where Engelhardt had placed it, on the stool. The next was his little inscription on the uppermost song. She knelt to read it again; when she had done so the two uncertain, left-handed, pencilled lines were wet and blotched with her tears, and she rose up knowing what she had never known before.

At eleven-thirty—she had set her heart upon that extra half hour if let alone—Mrs. Potter rattled the tea-tray against the sitting-room door and entered next moment. She found her mistress on the sofa certainly, but lying on her back and staring straight at the ceiling. Her face was very white and still, but she moved it a little as the door opened. She had not slept? Not a wink. Her book was lying in her lap; it had never been opened. Mrs. Potter was not slow to exhibit her disappointment, not to say her disgust. But Naomi sprang up with every sign of energy, and finished her tea in five minutes. In ten she had her horse saddled. In twelve she had cantered back to the veranda, and was receiving from Mrs. Potter the water-bag, the flask, and the packet of bread and meat.

"Have his room nice and ready for him," said the girl, excitedly, "and the kettle boiling, so that we may both have breakfast the instant we get in. It will be a pretty early breakfast, you'll see! Do you think you can do without sleep as long as I can?"

"Well, I know I sha'n't lie down while you're gone, miss."

"Then I'll be tremendously quick, I will indeed. I only wish I'd started long ago. The moon is splendid now. You can see miles—"

"Then look there, Miss Naomi!"

"Where?"

"Past the stables—across the paddock—toward the fence."

Naomi looked. A black figure was running toward them in the moonlight.

"Who can it be, Mrs. Potter? Not Mr. Engelhardt—"

"Who else?"

"But he is reeling and staggering! Could it be some drunken roustabout? And yet that's just his height—it must be—it is—thank God!"

Her curiosity first, and then her amazement, kept Naomi seated immovable in her saddle. She wondered later why she had not cantered to meet him. She did not stir even when his stertorous breathing came painfully to her ears. It was only when the quivering, spent, and speechless young man threw his arms across the withers of her horse, and his white face fell forward upon the mane, that Naomi silently detached the water-bag which she had strapped to her saddle, and held it to his lips with a trembling hand. At first he shook his head. Then he raised his wild eyes to hers with a piteously anxious expression.

"You have heard—that they are coming?"

"No—who?"

"You have heard, or why are you on horseback?"

"To look for you. I was on the point of starting. I made sure you must be bushed."

"I was. But I got to a camp. They looked after me; I am all right. And now they are coming in here—they're probably on their way!" Each little sentence came in a fresh gasp from his parched throat.

"But who?"

"Those two tramps who came the other day, and Simons, the ringer of the shed. Villains—villains every one!"

"Ah! And what do they want?"

"Can't you guess? The silver! The silver! That fat brute who insulted you so, who do you suppose he is? Tigerskin's mate—just out of prison—the man whose finger your father shot off ten years ago! You remember how he kept his hands in his pockets the other day? Well, that was the reason. Now there isn't a moment to lose. I listened to their plans. Half an hour ago—or it may be an hour—they lay down for a spell. They were drunk, but not very. They only meant to rest for a bit; then they're coming straight here. They left me tied up—they were going to bring me with them—I'll tell you afterward how I got loose. I daren't stop a moment, even to cut adrift their horses. I just bolted for the moon—I'd heard them say the station lay due east—and here I am. Thank God I've found you up and mounted! It couldn't have been better; it's providential. Now you mustn't get off at all; you must just ride right on to the shed."

"Must I?" said Naomi, with a tight lip and a keen eye, but a touch of the old banter in her tone.

"We could follow on foot. Meanwhile you would rouse them out at the shed—"

"And my silver?"

Engelhardt was silent. The girl leant forward in her saddle, and laid a hand upon his shoulder.

"No, no, Mr. Engelhardt! Captains don't quit their ships in such a hurry as all that. I'm captain here, and I'll stick to mine. It isn't only the silver. Still my father smelt powder for that silver, and the least I can do is to follow his lead."

She slid to the ground as she spoke.

"You will barricade yourself in the store?" said Engelhardt.

"Exactly. It was fixed up for this very kind of thing, after the first fuss with Tigerskin. They'll never get in."

"And you mean to stick to your guns inside?"

"To such as I have—most certainly."

"Then I mean to stick to you."

"Very well."

"But think—think before it's too late! They are devils, Miss Pryse—beasts! I have seen them and heard them. Better a hundred times be dead than at their mercy. For God's sake, take the horse before they are upon us!"

"I stop here," said Naomi, decidedly.

"Yet Mrs. Potter and I could hold the store as easily as you could. They shall not get your silver while I'm alive."

"My mind is made up," said the girl, in a voice which silenced his remonstrances; "but I agree with you that somebody ought to start off for the shed. I think that you should, Mr. Engelhardt, if you feel equal to it."

"Equal to it! It's so likely I would ride off and leave two women to the mercy of those brutes! If it really must be so, then I think the sooner we all three get into the store—"

It was Mrs. Potter who here put in her amazing word. While the young people stood and argued, her eyes had travelled over every point of the saddled horse. And now she proposed that she should be the one to ride to the shed for help.

"You!" the two cried in one breath, as they gazed at her ample figure.

"And why not?" said the hardy woman. "Wasn't I born and bred in the bush? Couldn't I ride—bareback, too—before either of you was born? I'm not so light as I used to be, and I haven't the nerve either; but what I have is all there in the hour of need, Miss Naomi. Let me go now. I'm ready this minute."

Naomi had seemed lost in thought.

"Very well!" cried she, whipping her eyes from the ground. "But you don't know the way to the shed, and I must make your directions pretty plain. Run to the back of the kitchen, Mr. Engelhardt, you'll see a lot of clothes-props. Bring as many as you can to the store veranda."

Engelhardt darted off upon his errand. Already they had wasted too many minutes in words. His brain was ablaze with lurid visions of the loathsome crew in Top Scrubby; of the murderous irruption imminent at any moment; of the unspeakable treatment to be suffered at those blood-stained hands—not only by himself—that mattered little—but by a woman—by Naomi of all women in the world. God help them both if the gang arrived before they were safe inside the store! But until the worst happened she need not know, nor should she guess, how bad that worst might be. Poor Rowntree's fate, and even his own ill-usage by those masterless men, were things which Engelhardt was not the man to tell to women in the hour of alarm. He was clear enough as to that; and having done up to this point all that a man could do, he jumped at the simple task imposed by Naomi, and threw himself into it with immense vigor and a lightened heart. As he dropped his first clothes-prop in the store veranda, Naomi and the housekeeper were still talking, though the latter was already huddled up in the saddle. When he got back with a second, both women were gone; with a third, Naomi was unlocking the store door; with the fourth and last, she had lit a candle inside, and was sawing one of the other props in two.

"That'll do," she said, as her saw ran through the wood. "Now hold this one up for me."

She pointed to another of the stout poles. She made him hold it with one end inside, and the other protruding through the opening. Then she made a mark on the prop at the level of the door, sawed it through at her mark, and cut down the other two in the same fashion. In less than five minutes the four poles had become eight, which cumbered the floor within. Then Naomi rose from her knees, flung the saw back into the tool-box, and made a final survey with the candle. A few flakes of sawdust lay about the shallow veranda. She fetched a broom from a corner of the store and whisked them away. Then she removed the key to the inside, and was about to lock the door upon herself and Engelhardt when he suddenly stopped her.

"Hold on!" he cried. "I want your boots."

"My boots?"

"Yes, those you've got on—with the dust on 'em, just as they are. They must be left outside your door, and your door must be locked; you must keep the key."

Naomi gave him a grateful, an admiring smile.

"That is a happy thought. I'll get it myself. While I'm gone you might fetch in the axe from the wood-heap; I'd almost forgotten it."

They ran off in different directions. Next minute they were both back in the store, Engelhardt with the axe. Naomi took it from him, and set it aside without a word. Her face was blanched.

"I heard something," she whispered. "I heard a cry. Oh, if they've seen me!"

"We'll lock the door as quietly as possible."

This was done.

"Now the props," said Naomi.

Engelhardt had guessed what they were for. He helped her to fix them, with one wedged between floor and counter, and the other pressing the heavy woodwork of the door. It now appeared how craftily Naomi had cut her timbers. They met the door, two at the top, two at the bottom, and four about the centre. Still the brave engineer was distressed.

"I meant to hammer them down," she murmured. "Now I daren't."

"We'll put all our weight on them instead," said Engelhardt. They did so with a will, until each prop had creaked in turn. Then they listened.

"Out with the light," said Naomi. "There are no windows to give us away—but still!"

He blew it out. As yet his own ears had heard nothing, and he was beginning to wonder whether Naomi had been deceived. They listened a little longer. Then she said:

"We're provisioned for a siege. Did you see the flask and things on the counter?"

"I did. How in the world did you find time to get them ready?"

"I had them ready before you came. They were for you."

The two were crouching close together between the props. It was a natural though not a necessary attitude. The moon was shining through the skylight upon one of the walls; the multifarious tins and bottles on the shelves made the most of the white light; and faint reflections reached the faces of Naomi and the piano-tuner—so close to each other, so pale, so determined, and withal so wistful as their eyes met. Engelhardt first looked his thanks, and then stammered them out in a broken whisper. Even as he did so the girl raised a finger to her lips.

"Hark! There they are."

"Yes, I hear them. They won't hear us yet a bit."

"They mustn't hear us at all; but off with your boots—we may have to move about."

She had already kicked off her shoes, and now, because he had only one of his own, she pulled off his boots with her two hands.

"You should not have done that!"

"Why not?"

"It's dreadful! Just as though you were my servant."

"Mr. Engelhardt, we must be everything to each other—"

She shot up her hand and ceased. The voices without were now distinguishable.

"To-night!" he muttered, bitterly, before heeding them.

Naomi, on the other hand, was at the last pitch of attention; but not to him. She inclined her head as she knelt to hear the better. The voices were approaching from one side.

"Ay, that's where he dropped—just there!" said one. It was Tigerskin's mate, Bill.

"Take the key from the door!" Engelhardt whispered to Naomi, who was the nearer it. They had forgotten to do this. For one wild moment the girl hesitated, then she cautiously reached out her hand and withdrew the key without a scratch.

"So this is the crib!" they heard Bo's'n say.

"The same old crib," said Bill. "Same as it was ten years ago, only plastered up a bit. I suppose it is locked, mate?"

The handle was tried. The door shook ever so little. The two inside gazed at the props and held their breath. If one of them should be shaken down!

"Ay, it's locked all right; and I reckon it's true enough about the girl sleeping with the key under her pillow, and all."

"Blast your reckonings!" said Bill. "Make sure the key ain't in the door on t'other side."

The thimbleful of starlit sky which Naomi had been watching for the last minute and a half was suddenly wiped away. She heard Bo's'n breathing hard as he stooped and peered. The key grew colder in her hand.

"No, there ain't no key, Bill."

"That's all right. They're both in their beds then, and that little suck-o'-my-thumb hasn't got here yet. When he does, God 'elp him!"

The voices were those of Bill and Bo's'n. For the moment these two seemed to be alone together.

"Ay, ay, we'd string the beggar up fast enough another time!"

"String him up? Yes, by his heels, and shoot holes through him while he dangled."

"Beginning where you don't kill. Holy smoke! but I wish he'd turn up now."

"So do I—the swine! But here comes the ringer. What cheer, matey?"

"It's right," said Simons. "The little devil's locked her door; but there are her boots outside, same as if she was stoppin' at a blessed 'otel. A fat lot she cared whether her precious pal was bushed or whether he wasn't! We thought you was telling us lies, mother, but, by cripes, you wasn't!"

"I should think not!" said a fourth voice. "She wouldn't believe he was lost, but I knew he was; so I just saddled the night-horse after she was in bed and asleep, and was going straight to the shed to raise a search-party!"

The pair within were staring at each other in dumb horror. That fourth voice was but too well known to them both. It was Mrs. Potter's.

CHAPTER XV

THE NIGHT ATTACK

"See here, mother!" said Bill. "There's one or two things we want to know. Spit out the truth, and that'll be all right. Tell us one lie, and there'll be an end of you. Understand?"

"I ought to."

"Right you are, then; now you know. What about this key?"

"She keeps it in her room."

"Under her pillow, eh?"

"That I can't say; but she will tell you."

"So we reckon. Now look here. Will you take your oath there's not another soul on the premises but you and her?"

The pair within again held their breath. They must be discovered; but the longer they could postpone it the shorter would be their danger. Mrs. Potter's heart was stout, however, and her tongue ready.

"I swear it," she cried, heartily.

"What makes you so cussed sure?"

"Why, it stands to reason. By rights there ought to be four of us. That's with Sam Rowntree and Mr. Engelhardt. Sam's gone off on his own hook somewhere"—Bill chuckled—"but nobody knows where. Mr. Engelhardt's lost, as I told you. So there's nobody left but mistress and me. How could there be?"

"I don't know or care a curse how there could be. I only know that if there is, you'll have a pill to take without opening your mouth for it. About this chap that's lost; you'll take your oath he didn't turn up before you left the station just now?"

"I told you he hadn't, as soon as ever you overtook me."

"You've got to swear it!" said Bill, savagely.

"I swore it then."

"So she did," said Simons, who had been grumbling openly during this cross-examination. "What's the good of going over the same track twice, mate? Let her give us the feed she promised, and then let's get to work."

"And so say I!" cried the Bo's'n.

"You shall have your supper in five minutes," said Mrs. Potter, "if you'll let me get it."

"All right, missus," said Bill, after a pause. "Only mind, if we catch you in any hanky-panky, by God I'll screw your neck till I put your face where your back-hair ought to be. Don't you dare get on the cross with us, or there'll be trouble! Come on, chaps. You show the way to the dining-room, mother, and light up; then we'll...."

The rest sounded indistinct in the store. The low crunching of the foot-falls in the sandy yard changed to a crisp clatter upon the homestead veranda. Naomi waited for that sign; then with a white face and eager hands she began to tear down, prop by prop, the barricade on which their very lives depended.

"She shall not suffer for this, whoever else does," she muttered. "At least she sha'n't suffer alone."

"You mean to open the door?"

"Yes, and catch her as she passes. To get to the kitchen she must pass close to the store. We'll open the door, and if she's wise she'll pass three or four times without turning her head; she'll wait till they're well at work; then she'll come back for something else—and slip in."

As she spoke Naomi went round to the gun-rack, took down the Winchester repeating-rifle, loaded it and came back to the front of the store. Then she directed Engelhardt to unlock the door, she helping him to be gentle with the key. The lock was let back by degrees. A moment later the door was wide open, with Naomi standing as in a frame, the Winchester in her hands.

The station-yard lay bathed and purified in the sweet moonlight. The well-palings opposite, and the barracks beyond, were as though newly painted white. The main building Naomi could not see without putting out her head, for it ran at right angles with the store, and she was standing well inside. But the night wind that blew freshly in her face bore upon it the noise of oaths and laughter from the dining-room, and presently that of footsteps, too. At this Naomi laid a finger on the trigger and stood like a rock, with the piano-tuner, like its shadow, at her side. But it was only Mrs. Potter who stepped into the moonlight. So far all was as Naomi had hoped and calculated.

But no further. When the poor soul saw the open door she stopped dead, hesitated half a second, and then ran like a heavy doe for it and Naomi. The latter had made adverse signals in vain. She drew aside to let the woman in, and was also in time to prevent Engelhardt from slamming the door. She shut it gently, turned the key with as much care as before, and with a sternly whispered "hush!" kept still to listen. The other two stood as silent, though Mrs. Potter, in the moment of safety and of reaction, was heaving and quivering all over, shedding tears like rain, and swaying perilously where she stood. But she kept her feet bravely during that critical minute; it was but one; the next, a shout of laughter from the distance made it clear that by a miracle the incident had passed unobserved and unsuspected.

"We may think ourselves lucky," said Naomi, severely. Next moment she had thrown her arms round the old woman's neck, and was covering her honest wrinkled face with her tears and kisses.

The practical Engelhardt was busily engaged in replacing the props against the door. His one hand made him slow at the work. Naomi was herself again in time to help him, and now there was sturdy Mrs. Potter to lend her weight. The supports were soon firmer than ever, with gimlets and bradawls driven into the door above those at the greatest slant, which were thus in most danger of being forced out of place. Then came a minute's breathing-space.

"I had just got through the first gate," Mrs. Potter was saying, "when I heard a galloping, and they were on me. Nay, Miss Naomi, it isn't anything to be proud of. I just said the first things that came into my head about you both; there was no time to think. It's only a mercy it's turned out so well."

"It was presence of mind," said Naomi. "We have scored an hour through it, and may another if they are long in missing you. If we can hold out till morning, someone may ride in from the shed. Don't you hear them talking still?"

"Yes; they're more patient than I thought they'd be."

"They think you're busy in the kitchen. When they find you're not, they'll waste their time looking all over the place for you—everywhere but here."

"Ay, but they'll come here in the end, and then may the Lord have mercy on our souls!"

"Come, come. They're not going to get in as easily as all that. And if they do, what with the Winchester—"

"Hush!" said Engelhardt. He was kneeling among the props, with his ear close to the bottom of the door.

All three listened. The voices were louder and more distinct. The men had come outside.

"I don't believe she's there at all," said one. "I see no light."

"Go you and have a look, Bo's'n. Prick the old squaw up with the p'int o' your knife. But if you find her trying to hide, or up to any o' them games, I'd slit her throat and save the barney."

"By cripes, so would I!"

"Ay, ay, messmates, but we'll see—we'll see."

All the voices were nearer now. Naomi had taken Mrs. Potter's hand, and was squeezing it white. For some moments they could make out nothing more. Bo's'n had evidently gone over to the kitchen. The other two were talking in low tones somewhere near the well-palings. Suddenly a muffled shout from the kitchen reached every ear.

"She's not here at all."

"Not there!"

"Come and look for yourselves."

"By gock," cried Bill, "let me just get my grip on her fat neck!"

A moment later the three could be heard ransacking the kitchen, and calling upon the fugitive to come out, with threats and imprecations most horrible to hear even in the distance; but as they drew nearer, working swiftly from out-building to out-building, like ferrets in a rabbit-warren, the ferocity of their language rose to such a pitch that the hunted woman within fell back faint and trembling upon the counter. Naomi was quick as thought with the flask; but her own cool hand and steady eyes were as useful as the brandy, and the fit passed as swiftly as it had come. While it lasted, however, the only one to follow every move outside was the assiduous Engelhardt. He had not yet risen from his knees; but he raised himself a little as Mrs. Potter stood upright again, supported by Naomi.

"It's all right," he whispered. "They've no idea where you are. Simons has had a look in the barracks, and Bo's'n in the pines. But they've given you up now. They're holding a council of war within five yards of us!"

"Let's listen," said Naomi. "Their language won't kill us."

They had quite given up Mrs. Potter. This was evident from the tail-end of a speech in which Bill bitterly repented not having "stiffened" both her and Engelhardt at sight.

"As for getting to the shed," said Simons, who was the obvious authority on this point, "that'll take her a good hour and a half on foot. It'd be a waste of time and trouble to ride after her, though I'd like to see Bill at work on her—I should so! If she had her horse, it'd be another thing."

"Ay, ay," cried the Bo's'n. "Let the old gal rip."

Bill had been of the same opinion a moment before; but this indecent readiness to be beaten by an old woman was more than he could share or bear. He told his mate so in highly abusive terms. They retorted that he was beaten by that same old woman himself. Bill was not so sure of that; what about the bedroom with the boots outside? Nobody had looked in there.

A brisk debate ensued, in which the voice of Simons rose loudest. Bill, on the other hand, spoke in a much lower tone than usual; his words did not penetrate into the store; it was as though they were meant not to. And yet it was Bill who presently cried aloud:

"Then that's agreed. We all three go together to rouse her up anyhow, whether the old gal's there or whether she isn't. Come on!"

Apparently they went then and there.

"Nice for me!" whispered Naomi. "Nice for us both, Mrs. Potter, if we weren't safe—"

A bovine roar seemed to burst from their very midst. It was Bill outside the door.

"Tricked 'em, by God!" he yelled. "Here they are. Never mind that room. I tell you they're here—both of 'em; I heard 'em whispering."

"Bill, you're a treat," said the Bo's'n, running up. "I never saw such a man—"

"Where's Simons?"

"He was bound to have a look for hisself. Here he comes. Well, messmate, where is she?"

"Not there," cried Simons, with an oath. "The room's as empty as we are. There's been no one in it all night."

Bill laughed.

"I knew that, matey. You might have saved yourself the trouble when I sang out. She's—in—here." And he kicked the store door three times with all his might.

"Who is?" said Simons.

"Both on 'em. What did I tell you? They started whisperin' the moment they thought we'd sheered off."

"They're not whisperin' now," said Simons, at the keyhole. "By cripes, let's burst the door in!"

"Hold on," said Bill. "If they're not born fools they'll listen to reason. Out o' the light, matey. See here, ladies, if you walk out now you may live to spin the yarn, but if you don't—" He broke away into nameless blasphemies.

The cruel voice came hoarse and hot through the keyhole. Engelhardt opened his mouth to reply, but Naomi clapped a warm palm upon it, and with the other hand signalled silence to Mrs. Potter.

"We've given 'em their chance," said Bill, after a pause. "Come on, chaps. One, two, all together—now!"

There was a stampede of feet in the shallow veranda, and then a thud and a crash, as the three men hurled themselves against the door. But for their oaths outside, in the store it was as though nothing had happened. Not a timber had given, not a prop was out of place. Naomi's white face wore a smile, which, however, was instantly struck out by a loud report and a flash through the keyhole.

Engelhardt crouched lower, picked something from the floor, and passed it up to Naomi in his open hand.

She carried it into the moonlight. It was a wisp of the musician's long hair, snipped out by the bullet.

They stood aside from the keyhole. More bullets came through, but all at the same angle. The women caught up a sack of flour, rolled it over the counter, and with Engelhardt's help jammed it between the props, so that the top just covered the keyhole. Next moment there was a rush against the door, and for the second time all the harm was done to the besiegers, not the besieged.

"We'll be black and blue before we've anything to show for it!" they heard the Bo's'n groaning.

"There's more than women in this," said Bill. "There's that spawn that I should have strung up if it hadn't been for you two white-feathers. It's yourselves you've got to thank for this. I might have known it the moment I caught sight o' that lump o' lard on horseback. The swine's been in here all the time!"

"He has!" shouted Engelhardt at the top of his excited voice; "and it's where you'll never get, not a man of you! You take that from me!"

For a short space there was a hush outside. Then arose such a storm of curses and foul threats that the women within put their fingers in their ears. When they withdrew them, all was silence once more, and this time it lasted.

"They must have gone for something!" exclaimed Naomi.

"They have," said the piano-tuner, coolly. "A battering-ram!"

"Then now's our time," cried the girl. "It's absurd to think of our being cooped up here with any quantity of fire-arms, and no chance of using one of them! First we must light up. Chop that candle in two, Mrs. Potter. It'll see us through to daybreak, and there's nothing to keep dark any longer, so the more light now the better. Ah, here's the tool-box, and yes! here's the brace and bits. Now this is my little plan."

She took the brace, fitted it with the largest bit, and was making for the door.

"What are you going to do?" said Engelhardt.

"Make a loop-hole to fire through."

"And for them to fire through, too!"

"Well, that can't be helped."

"Excuse me, I think it can. I've been puzzling the thing out for the last hour. I've a better plan than that!"

"Let me hear it."

"A tomahawk!"

She gave him one from the tool-box.

"May I hack the roofing a bit?"

"As much as ever you like."

"Now a pile of boxes—here—just at the left of the door—and four feet high."

The women had it ready in a twinkling. They then helped him to clamber to the top—no easy matter with an arm that was not only useless, but an impediment at every turn. When he stood at his full height his head touched the corrugated iron some twenty inches from the obtuse angle between roof and wall.

He reached out his hand for the tomahawk, and at the height of his eyes he hacked a slit in the iron, prising the lower lip downward until he could see well out into the yard. Then, a handbreadth above the angle, he made a round hole with the sipke of the tomahawk, and called for a revolver. Naomi produced a pair. He took one, and worked the barrel in the round hole until it fitted loosely enough to permit of training. Then he looked down. There was no sign of the thieves.

"Have you plenty of cartridges, Miss Pryse?"

"Any amount."

"Well, I don't expect to spill much blood with them; but, on the other hand, I'm not likely to lose any myself." The work and the danger had combined to draw his somewhat melancholy spirit out of itself. Or perhaps it was not the danger itself, but the fact that he shared it with Naomi Pryse. Whatever the cause, the young man was more light-hearted than was his wont. "They'll fire at the spot I fire from," he explained, with a touch of pride; "they'll never think of my eyes being two feet higher up, and their bullets must strike the roof at such an angle that no charge on earth would send them through. Mind, it'll be the greatest fluke if I hit them; but they aren't to know that; and at any rate I may keep them out of worse mischief for a time."

"You may and you will," said Naomi, enthusiastically. "But still we shall want my loop-hole!"

"Why so?"

"The veranda!"

For some moments Engelhardt said nothing. When at last he found his voice it was to abuse himself and his works with such unnecessary violence that again that soft warm palm lay for an instant across his lips. His pride in his own ingenuity had been cruelly humbled, for he had to confess that he had entirely forgotten to reckon with the store-veranda, a perfect shelter against even the deadliest fusillade from his position.

"Very well," he cried at last. "We'll drill a hole through the door, but we must drill it near the top, and at an angle, so that they can't put a bullet through it at a distance."

"Then let me do it," said Naomi. She sprang upon the flour-bag, and the hole was quickly made. Still the men did not return. "Lucky thing I remembered the axe in time!" she continued, remaining where she was. "They would have hacked in the door in no time with that. I say, Mr. Engelhardt, this is my post. I mean to stick here."

"Never!" he cried.

"But you can't work both revolvers."

"Well, then, let us change places. You'll probably shoot straighter than I should. I'll stand on the flour-bag with the barrel of the other revolver through the hole you've made. If any one of them gets in a line with it—well, there'll be a villain less!"

"And Mrs. Potter shall load for us," cried Naomi. "Do you know how?"

"Can't say I do, miss."

"Then I'll show you."

This was the work of a moment. The old bush-woman was handy enough, and cool enough too, now that she was getting used to the situation. It was her own idea to bring round the storekeeper's tall stool, to plant it among the props, within reach of Naomi on the boxes and of Engelhardt on the flour-bag, and to perch herself on its leather top with the box of cartridges in her lap. Thus prepared and equipped, this strange garrison waited for the next assault.

"Here they come," cried Naomi at last, with a sudden catch in her voice. "They're carrying a great log they must have fished out from the very bottom of the wood-heap. All the top part of the heap was small wood, and I guess they've wasted some more time in hunting for the axe. But here they are!" She pushed her revolver through the slit in the roof, and the sharp report rang through the store.

"Hit anybody?" said Engelhardt next moment.

"No. They're stopping to fire back. Ah, you were right."

As she spoke there was a single report, followed by three smart raps on the sloping roof. The bullet had ricochetted like a flat stone flung upon a pond. Another and another did the same, and Naomi answered every shot.

"For God's sake take care!" cried the piano-tuner.

"I am doing so."

"Hit any one yet?"

"Not yet; it's impossible to aim; and they've never come nearer than the well-palings. Ah!"

"What now?"

"They're charging with the log."

Engelhardt slipped his revolver into his pocket, and grasped the shelf that jutted out over the lintel. He felt that the shock would be severe, and so it was. It came with a rush of feet and a volley of loud oaths—a crash that smashed the lock and brought three of the clothes-props clattering to the ground. But those secured by gimlet and bradawl still held; and though the lower part of the door had given an inch the upper fitted as close as before, and the hinges were as yet uninjured.

"One more does it!" cried Bill. "One more little rush like the last, and then, by God, if we don't make the three of you wish you was well dead, send me to quod again for ten year! Aha, you devil with the pistol! Very nice you'd got it arranged, but it don't cover us here. No, no, we've got the bulge on you now, you swine you! And you can't hit us, neither! We're going to give you one chance more when we've got our breath—just one, and then—"

By holding on to the shelf when the crash came Engelhardt had managed to stand firm on the flour-bag. Seeing that the door still held, though badly battered, he had put his eye to the loop-hole bored by Naomi, and it had fallen full on Bill. A more bestial sight he had never seen, not even in the earlier hours of that night. The bloated face was swimming with sweat, and yet afire with rage and the lust for blood. The cross-eyes were turned toward the holes in the roof, hidden from them by the veranda, and the hairy fist with the four fingers was being savagely shaken in the same direction. The man was standing but a foot from the door, and when Engelhardt removed his eye and slipped his pistol-barrel in the place, he knew that it covered his midriff, though all that he could see through the half-filled hole was a fragment of the obscene, perspiring face. It was enough to show him the ludicrous change of expression which followed upon a sudden lowering of the eyes and a first glimpse of the protruding barrel. Without a moment's hesitation Engelhardt pressed the trigger while Bill was stupidly repeating:

"And then—and then—"

A flash cut him short, and as the smoke and the noise died away, Engelhardt, removing the pistol once more and applying his eye, saw the wounded brute go reeling and squealing into the moonshine with his hand to his middle and the blood running over it. To the well-palings he reeled, dropping on his knees when he got there, but struggling to his feet and running up and down and round and round like a mad bull, still screaming and blaspheming at the top of his voice, and with the blood bubbling over both his hands, which never ceased to hug his wound. His mates rushed up to him, but he beat them off, cursing them, spitting at them, and covering them with blood as he struck at them with his soaking fists. It was their fault. They should have let him have his way. He would have done for that hell-begotten swine who had now done for him. It was they who had killed him—his own mates—and he told them so with shrieks and curses, varied with sobs and tears, and yet again with wild shots from a revolver which he plucked from his belt. But he dropped the pistol after madly discharging it twice, and clapping his hand to his middle, as though he could only live by pressing the wound with all his force, he rushed after them, foaming at the mouth and squirting blood at every stride. At last he seemed to trip, and he fell forward in a heap, but turned on one side, his knees coming up with a jerk, his feet treading the air as though running still. And for some seconds they so continued, like the screws of a foundering steamer; then he rolled over heavily; his two companions came up at a walk; one of them touched him with his foot; and Engelhardt stepped down from the flour-bag with a mouth that had never relaxed, and a frown that had never gone.

Naomi was no longer standing on the boxes; but she was sitting on them, with her face in her hands; and in the light of the two candle-ends, Mrs. Potter was watching her with a white dazed face.

"Cheer up!" said Engelhardt. "The worst is over now."

"Is he dead?" said Naomi, uncovering her face.

"As dead as a man can be."

"And you shot him?"

She knew that he had; but the thing seemed incredible as she sat and looked at him; and by the time it came fully home to her, the little musician was inches taller in her eyes.

"Yes, I shot the brute; and I'll shoot that shearer, too, if I get half a chance."

Naomi felt nervous about it, and sufficiently shocked. She was dubiously remarking that they had not committed murder, when she was roughly interrupted.

"Haven't they!"

"Whom have they murdered?"

"You'll see."

"I know!" cried Mrs. Potter, with sudden inspiration; but even as they looked at her, a voice was heard shouting from a respectful distance outside.

"We're going," it cried. "We've had enough of this, me and Simons have. Only when they find that chap in the paddock, recollect it was Bill that hung him. But for us he'd have hung you, too!"

They listened very closely, but they heard no more. Then Naomi stood up to look through the slit in the roof.

"The yard is empty," she cried. "Their horses are gone! Oh, Mr. Engelhardt—Mr. Engelhardt—we are saved!"

CHAPTER XVI

IN THE MIDST OF DEATH

The candle-ends had burnt out in the store; the moon no longer shone in through the skylight; but the latter was taking new shape, and a harder outline filled with an iron-gray that whitened imperceptibly, like a man's hair. The strange trio within sat still and silent, watching each other grow out of the gloom like figures on a sensitive film. The packet of meat and bread was reduced to a piece of paper and a few crumbs; the little flask was empty, and the water-bag half its former size; but now that all was over, the horror of the night lay heavier upon them than during the night itself. It was Naomi who broke the long silence at last.

"They have evidently gone," she said. "Don't you think we might venture now?"

"It is for you to decide," said Engelhardt.

"What do you think, Mrs. Potter?"

"If you ask me, Miss Naomi, I think it's beneath us to sit here another minute for a couple of rascals who will be ten miles away by this time."

"Then let us go. I will take the Winchester, and if they are still about we must just slip in again quicker than we came out. But I think it's good enough to chance."

"So do I," said the piano-tuner, "most decidedly."

"Then down with the props. They have served us very well, and no mistake! You must keep them in your kitchen, Mrs. Potter, as a trophy for all time."

The old woman made no reply. Of what she was thinking none ever knew. Her life had run in a narrow, uneventful groove. Its sole adventure was probably the one now so nearly at an end. Ten years ago she had been ear-witness of a somewhat similar incident. And now she had played a part, and no small part, in another and a worse. At her age she might have come out shaken and shattered to the verge of imbecility, after such a night. Or she might have felt inordinately proud of her share in the bushrangers' repulse. But when at last the battered door stood wide open, and the keen morning air chilled their faces, and the red morning sky met their eyes, the old woman looked merely sad and thoughtful, and years older since the day before. Her expression touched Naomi. Once more she threw her young arms about the wrinkled neck, and left kisses upon the rough cheek, and words of grateful praise in the old ears. Meanwhile Engelhardt had pushed past them both and marched into the middle of the yard.

"It's all right, I think," said he, standing purposely between the women and the hideous corpse by the well-palings. "Yes, the coast is clear. But there's the horse you rode, Mrs. Potter, and Bill's horse, too, apparently, tied side by side to the fence."

"May God forgive them all," said Mrs. Potter, gravely, as she walked across the yard at Naomi's side.

They were the last words she ever uttered. As she spoke, the crack of a rifle, with the snap of a pistol before and after, cut the early stillness as lightning cuts the sky. Naomi wheeled round and levelled her Winchester at the two men who were running with bent backs from a puff of smoke to a couple of horses tethered among the pines beyond kitchen and wood-heap. She sighted the foremost runner, but never fired. A heavy fall at her side made her drop the Winchester and turn sharply round. It was Mrs. Potter. She was lying like a log, with her brave old eyes wide open to the sky, and a bullet in her heart.

"Take me away," said the girl, faintly, as she got up from her knees. "I can bear no more."

"There are the horses," answered the piano-tuner, pointing to the two that were tied up to the fence. "I should dearly like to give chase!"

"No, no, no!" cried Naomi, in an agony. "Hasn't there been enough bloodshed for one night? We will ride straight to the shed. They have taken the very opposite direction. Let us start at once!"

"In an instant," he said, and ran indoors for something to throw over the dead woman. The girl was again kneeling beside her, when he came back with a table-cloth. And she was crying bitterly when, a minute later, he slipped his left hand under her foot and helped her into the saddle.

They never drew rein until the long, low wool-shed was well in sight. The sun was up. It was six o'clock. They could see the shearers swarming to the shed like bees to a hive. The morning air was pungent as spiced wine. Some color had come back to Naomi's cheeks, and it was she who first pulled up, forcing Engelhardt to do the same.

"Friday morning!" she said, walking her horse. "Can you realize that you only came last Saturday night?"

"I cannot."

"No more can I! We have been through so much—"

"Together."

"Together and otherwise. I think you must have gone through more than I can guess, when you were lost in Top Scrubby, and when you fell in with those fiends. Will you tell me all about it some time or other?"

"I'm afraid there will be no opportunity," said Engelhardt, speaking with unnatural distinctness. "I must be off to-day."

"To-day!"

Her blank tone thrilled him to the soul.

"Of course," he said, less steadily. "Why not? I did my best to get away the night before last. Thank God I didn't succeed in that!"

"Why did you go like that?"

"You know why."

"I know why! What do you mean? How can I know anything?"

"Very easily," he bitterly replied, staring rigidly ahead with his burning face. "Very easily indeed, when I left you that letter!"

"What letter, Mr. Engelhardt?"

"The awful nonsense I was idiot enough to slip into your book!"

"The book I was reading?"

"Yes."

"Then I have never had your letter. I haven't opened that book since the day before yesterday, though more than once I have taken it up with the intention of doing so."

"Well, thank Heaven for that!"

"But why?"

"Because I said—"

"Well, what did you say?"

She caught his bridle, and, by stopping both horses, forced him to face her at last.

"Surely you can guess? I had just got to know about Tom Chester, and I felt there was no hope for me, so I thought—"

"Stop! what had you got to know about Tom Chester, please?"

"That he cared for you."

"Indeed! To me that's a piece of news. Mind, I care for him very much as a friend—as a hand."

"Then you don't—"

"No, indeed I don't."

"Oh, Naomi, what am I to say? In that letter I said it all—when I had no hope in my heart. And now—"

"And now you have called that letter awful nonsense, and yourself an idiot for writing it!"

She was smiling at him—her old, teasing smile—across the gap between their horses. But his eyes were full of tears.

"Oh, Naomi, you know what I meant!"

"And I suppose it has never occurred to you what I mean?"

He stared at her open-eyed.

"Will you marry me?" he blurted out.

"We'll see about that," said Naomi, as he took her hand and they rode onward with clasped fingers. "But I'll tell you what I am on to do. I'm on to put Taroomba in the market this very day, and to back you for all that it fetches. After that there's Europe—your mother—Milan—and anything you like, my dear fellow, for the rest of our two lives."

E. W. Hornung – A Short Biography

Ernest William Hornung was born on 7th June 1866 at Cleveland Villas, Marton, Middlesbrough. He was the third son, and youngest of eight children, to John Peter Hornung and his wife Harriet née Armstrong.

By the age of 13 Hornung had joined St Ninian's Preparatory School in Moffat, Dumfriesshire before enrolling at the exclusive Uppingham School, in Rutland, in 1880.

Hornung suffered from a general state of bad health, including asthma and poor eyesight but managed to be well-liked at school and to develop a life-long passion of cricket. He loved to play despite the obvious fact that his talents were rather limited.

At 17 his health worsened, and he left Uppingham to travel to Australia, where a sunnier climate was deemed to be better for his various ailments.

Upon arriving he worked as a tutor to the Parsons family in Mossgiel, in New South Wales. As well as teaching he spent time working in remote sheep stations in the outback and began to contribute materials to the weekly magazine; The Bulletin. It was also at this time that he began work on his first novel.

After two years of very valuable life experiences Hornung returned to England in February 1886, a few months before the death of his father, in November, whose deteriorating business interests had become a constant worry.

Hornung found work in London as a journalist and story writer. In 1887 he published his first story under his own name, 'Stroke of Five', which appeared in Belgravia magazine. His work as a journalist coincided with the reign of terror brought about by Jack the Ripper's grisly murders. From this Hornung developed an interest in criminal behaviour.

He had completed the manuscript of the novel he brought back from Australia and, between July and November 1890, the story, 'A Bride from the Bush', was published in five parts in the respected Cornhill Magazine. It was released later that year in book form. This, his first novel, was well received by critics.

Hoping to further his talents in cricket Hornung, in 1891, became a member of two cricket clubs: the Idlers, whose members included Arthur Conan Doyle and Jerome K. Jerome, and the Strand club.

Hornung knew Doyle's sister, Constance ('Connie') from when he had visited Portugal. Connie was described as attractive, "with pre-Raphaelite looks ... the most sought-after of the Doyle daughters".

They were married on 27th September 1893, although Doyle was not at the wedding and relations between the two writers were occasionally difficult. The Hornung's had their only child, a son, Arthur Oscar (but always called just Oscar), in 1895.

In 1894 Doyle and Hornung began work on a play for Henry Irving, on the subject of boxing; Doyle was, at first, eager to begin and paid Hornung a £50 advance but then withdrew before the first act had been completed: the play was never finished.

Like Hornung's first novel, 'Tiny Luttrell' had Australia as a backdrop and the device of an Australian woman in a culturally alien environment. This theme ran through his next four novels: 'The Boss of Taroomba' (1894), 'The Unbidden Guest' (1894), 'Irralie's Bushranger' (1896), in this Hornung introduced the character of Stingaree, an Oxford-educated, Australian gentleman thief. In 'The Rogue's March' (1896) Hornung began to show a growing fascination with the motivation behind criminal behaviour and was sympathetic to the criminal hero as a victim of events. It was different thinking but caused some consternation for others.

In 1898 Hornung's mother died and he dedicated his next book, a series of short stories; Some Persons Unknown, to her memory.

Later that year Hornung and Connie spent six months in Posillipo, Italy. An account of this trip was published in the May 1899 issue of the Cornhill Magazine.

The fictional character Stingaree was re-written to become his most famous creation; A. J. Raffles; the gentleman thief, first used in six short stories published in 1898 in Cassell's Magazine. Modelled on George Cecil Ives, a Cambridge-educated criminologist and talented cricketer who, like Raffles, lived in the Albany, a gentlemen's only residence in Mayfair. The first tale of the series 'In the Chains of Crime' was published in June that year, titled 'The Ides of March'.

Another account adds to the richness by asserting that Raffles and his sidekick, Bunny Manders, were based not only on Doyle's Holmes and Watson but also on his friends Oscar Wilde and his lover, Lord Alfred Douglas. Whatever the exact amalgam the characters were warmly embraced by the reading public who turned it into both a popular and financial success, although some critics echoed Doyle's own fears of the dubious nature of a criminal being used as a hero.

In early 1899, the Hornung's returned to London, and resided in Pitt Street, West Kensington, for the next six years.

After publishing two novels, 'Dead Men Tell No Tales' (1899) and 'Peccavi' (1900), Hornung published a second collection of Raffles stories, 'The Black Mask', in 1901. The critics again complained about the criminal aspect. The public who bought them had no such qualms.

In 1903 Hornung collaborated with Eugène Presbrey to write a four-act play, 'Raffles, The Amateur Cracksman', which was based on two previously published short stories, 'Gentlemen and Players' and 'The Return Match'. The play was first performed at the Princess Theatre, New York, on 27th October 1903 and ran for 168 performances.

In 1905, after publishing four other books in the interim, Hornung brought back the character Stingaree. Later that year, in response to public demand he published a third collection of Raffles stories in 'A Thief in the Night', in which Manders relates some of the earlier adventures he had had with Raffles.

In 1909 the final Raffles story was published, the full-length novel 'Mr. Justice Raffles'. It was poorly received. The Observer reviewer asking if "Hornung is perhaps a little tired of Raffles".

It seems not. That same year he partnered with Charles Sansom for the play 'A Visit From Raffles', which was performed in November that year at the Brixton Empress Theatre, London.

Hornung turned away from Raffles thereafter, and in February 1911 published 'The Camera Fiend', a thriller whose narrator is an asthmatic cricket enthusiast and his attempts to photograph the soul as it leaves the body. This was followed by 'Fathers of Men' (1912) and 'The Thousandth Woman' (1913) before 'Witching Hill' (1913), a collection of eight short stories in which he introduced the characters Uvo Delavoye and the narrator Gillon. In 1914 his fictional works ceased with 'The Crime Doctor'.

His son, Oscar, left Eton College in 1914, and was due to proceed to King's College, Cambridge later that year. However, the terrors of WWI were about to unleash themselves all over Europe. Oscar volunteered, and was commissioned into the Essex Regiment. He was killed, aged a mere 20, at the Second Battle of Ypres on 6th July 1915.

Although heartbroken Hornung edited and issued privately a collection of Oscar's letters home under the title 'Trusty and Well Beloved', in 1916.

Around this time Hornung himself joined an anti-aircraft unit. He also joined the YMCA and did volunteer work in England for soldiers on leave. In March 1917 he visited France, writing a poem about his experience afterwards—something he had been doing more frequently since Oscar's death—and a collection of his war poetry, 'Ballad of Ensign Joy', was published later that year.

In July 1917 Hornung's poem, 'Wooden Crosses', was published in The Times, and in September, 'Bond and Free' appeared. A few months later he was accepted as a volunteer in a YMCA canteen and library just a few miles behind the Front Line.

Hornung was concerned about support for pacifism among troops and wrote to Connie about it. She spoke to Doyle and, rather than discussing it with Hornung, he informed the military authorities. Hornung was naturally angered by Doyle's action and relations between the two men were further strained as a result. He continued to work at the library until a German offensive overran the British positions and he was forced to retreat, firstly to Amiens and then, in April, back to England. He stayed in England until November 1918, when he again took up his YMCA duties, establishing a rest hut and library in Cologne.

In 1919 Hornung's account of his time spent in France, 'Notes of a Camp-Follower on the Western Front', was published. Doyle later wrote of the book that "there are parts of it which are brilliant in their vivid portrayal". That year Hornung also published his third and final volume of poetry, 'The Young Guard'.

Hornung finished his YMCA work and returned to England in early 1919. He worked on a new novel but was hampered by poor health. But Connie's was of greater concern. In February 1921 they took a holiday in the south of France to recuperate. Whilst travelling there on the train Hornung fell ill with a chill that progressed to influenza and finally pneumonia.

Ernest William Hornung died on 22nd March 1921, aged 54.

He was buried in Saint-Jean-de-Luz, in the south of France, in a grave adjacent to that of George Gissing.

E. W. Hornung – A Concise Bibliography

Periodicals
Stroke of Five (1887, Belgravia)
Spoilt Negative (1887, Belgravia)
Nettleship's Score (January 1890, Cornhill Magazine)

A Bride From the Bush (5 Parts. July-Nov, Cornhill Magazine, 1890)
Thunderbolt's Mate (4 Parts. March 1892, Chambers's Journal)
Kenyon's Innings (April 1892, Longman's Magazine)
The Burrawurra Brand (November 1893, The Idler)
The Unbidden Guest (6 Parts. May-Oct 1894, Longman's Magazine)
The Governess at Greenbush (4 parts. February 1895, Chambers's Journal)
After the Fact (3 Parts. January 1896, Chambers's Journal)
The Ides of March (June 1898, Cassell's Magazine)
A Villa in a Vineyard (May 1899, Cornhill Magazine)
No Sinecure: More Adventures of the Amateur Cracksman (January 1901, Scribner's Magazine)
A Jubilee Present: More Adventures of the Amateur Cracksman (February 1901, Scribner's Magazine)
The Fate of Faustina: More Adventures of the Amateur Cracksman (March 1901, Scribner's Magazine)
The Last Laugh: More Adventures of the Amateur Cracksman (April 1901, Scribner's Magazine)
To Catch a Thief: More Adventures of the Amateur Cracksman (May 1901, Scribner's Magazine)
An Old Flame: More Adventures of the Amateur Cracksman (June 1901, Scribner's Magazine)
The Wrong House: More Adventures of the Amateur Cracksman (Sept 1901, Scribner's Magazine)
Chrystal's Century (June 1903, Atlantic Monthly)
Charles Reade (June 1921, London Mercury)

Novels and Short Story Collection
A Bride from the Bush (1890) Novel
Under Two Skies (1892) Short story collection
Tiny Luttrell (1893) Novel; two volumes
The Boss of Taroomba (1894) Novel
The Unbidden Guest (1894) Novel
Irralie's Bushranger (1896) Novel
The Rogue's March: A Romance (1896) Novel
My Lord Duke (1897) Novel
Some Persons Unknown (1898) Short story collection
Young Blood (1898) Novel
The Amateur Cracksman (1899) Short story collection
Dead Men Tell No Tales (1899) Novel
The Belle of Toorak (1900) Novel; published in the US as The Shadow of a Man
Peccavi (1900) Novel
The Black Mask (1901) Short story collection; republished as Raffles: Further Adventures of the Amateur
Cracksman
At Large (1902) Novel
The Shadow of the Rope (1902) Novel
Denis Dent: A Novel (1903) Novel
No Hero (1903) Novel
Stingaree (1905) Novel
A Thief in the Night (1905) Short story collection; republished as A Thief in the Night: Further Adventures
of A. J. Raffles, Cricketer and Cracksman
Raffles: The Amateur Cracksman (1906) Short story collection; stories taken from The Amateur
Cracksman and The Black Mask
Mr. Justice Raffles (1909) Novel
The Camera Fiend (1911) Novel

Fathers of Men (1912) Novel
The Thousandth Woman (1913) Novel
Witching Hill (1913) Short story collection
The Crime Doctor (1914) Short story collection
Old Offenders and a Few Old Scores (Published posthumously) Short story collection

Plays
Raffles, The Amateur Cracksman (27th October 1903) By Hornung and Eugéne Presbrey; first performed
at the Princess Theatre, New York
Stingaree, the Bushranger (1st February 1908) First performed at the Queen's Theatre, London
A Visit From Raffles (1st November 1909) By Hornung and Charles Sansom; first performed at the
Brixton Empress Theatre, London

Non-Fiction
'Trusty and Well Beloved', The Little Record of Arthur Oscar Hornung (1915) Privately published
Notes of a Camp-Follower on the Western Front (1919)

Poetry
Ballad of Ensign Joy (1917)
Wooden Cross (1918)
The Young Guard (1919)